CONCRETE BAYOU

BRIDGETT MCGILL

THE QUEEN WITHIN

This book is dedicated to every woman that has ever experienced any type of verbal, mental, sexual or physical abuse, or any form of trafficking at the hands of a man or another woman and came out on the other side.
You are a survivor, a curse breaker, an agent of cease and assist.
Tell your story so that someone else can know and believe they too can overcome.
Selah

ACKNOWLEDGMENTS

First and foremost, the Most High God must and always will be acknowledged. It was HE who placed this book on my heart. It is from his Word, that this contemporary version of the story of Esther was born. How excited I am to release a version of this book that we can relate to in this day and age. May every reader be blessed and venture back to the biblical story of our beloved Esther and understand the warfare she was truly fighting.

I would like to acknowledge my friend, Yolanda Watson. After reading the first chapter, she physically stood and gave me a hug and said, "Sis, finish this." I accepted her encouragement and the challenge. Thank you Queen.

I will always acknowledge my editor, Naleighna Kai, for her constant push and teaching. This will be my first bestseller, because of her never-ending drive for excellence.

To my daughters – Kwaanza and Kayla my forever 'Hype Men'. Thanks for constantly
pushing me to complete this project and speaking into existence that this book will become a
movie. We rocking and rolling till the wheels fall off. I love y'all and my grandbabies so much!

With Love and Gratitude,
Queen Bea.

PROLOGUE

"*N*ow, why do you want to mess up a good thing?" The tall, well-dressed man pretended to pout. "Haven't I been good to you these eight years, Ms. Margaret?"

"Yes, you have Vik. You're the reason I'm able to retire at sixty-two instead of sixty-five and for that, I thank you."

The pudgy woman unhooked the rhinestone clasp that held together a soft pink jacket with the matching skirt; her off-white camisole exposing a plump belly. She then offered a manila envelope and placed the one he gave her inside her open purse.

"And my condolences to you for losing your husband." He nodded towards her, lightly touching his chest.

"Thank you so very much. I wish I could say that I miss him, truth is the only thing I won't miss is him always hounding me for extra money to pay his gambling debts." She shrugged, leaning against the black marble desk. Her guest let out a slight chuckle.

"I know why you're making that face. And as always, I thank you for the extras you gave me when I needed to bail him out. But such is life and we're moving on." His smile remained in agreement with her statement.

"Here are the last three girls that you might be interested in. They're right here in the city, easy to get to, no helicopter parents."

Margaret settled in the chair next to Vik, crossing her legs at the ankles as she leaned towards him. "Vik you've been at this, what, ten years now? How much longer are you going to run the Bayou? You've been the President of the Towers for twelve years. I've been hearing the higher-ups are looking to promote you because of your successful track record."

Viktor Batista smiled and the features of his dangerously handsome face took on a pleasant edge. "We'll see. I have my sights set on seats at some bigger tables, but you know my love for Bayou is something special."

The older woman laughed as she relaxed against the back of the chair, causing Viktor's expression to darken. "Selling ass is what you consider special, hunh?"

"What I sell put both of your children through college, and what did you just say? He stood and placed the envelope in his briefcase and turned towards the door to leave.

"You're retiring three years earlier than planned and all of your beloved husband's business, shall we say, was always taken care of. So let's not laugh now."

Margaret didn't move her head as she spoke. "All things good or bad at some point must come to an end." Her heavy laughter followed as he swept from her office.

Mrs. Margaret Wilkerson had been working for the Department of Social Services for twenty-seven years and held the director's position for the past ten. Her partnership with Vik had not only covered her children's expenses, but most of her recently deceased husband's gambling losses. She and Viktor Batista met at a political function held by the previous Mayor.

After eavesdropping on a conversation between Viktor and a local alderman regarding setting up a date at the Bayou, she scheduled a meeting with him. After hinting that she knew of the Alderman's reputation for spending time with escorts, she made him an offer he couldn't refuse; direct access to girls who came across her desk that were in some form of crisis. The rest was history. Besides basic information, she supplied information that helped manipulate their young minds. The girls were run-aways, orphans, revolving in foster care or in counseling because of trouble with their parents. Viktor preferred getting girls this way since it was easy to take them 'off the grid.' Most times, no one would look for them. And when someone did, he had police in his pocket that could make them go away.

The girls were easy to convince that his way was a better situation. It was also less risky than the 'guerilla pimping' method that he started with ten years ago. With Wilkerson's retirement, the "easy access" cord was being snipped. He was going to miss the cord more than he missed the pesty woman and her loud perfume.

Vik let out a sigh and smoothed the front of his blazer as he stepped into the underground parking garage. There was always demand in the bayou for one more girl. He simply needed a new plan.

CHAPTER 1

"**W**here am I? Open this damn door." An unfamiliar girl's voice echoed around Hadassah Colton's head. Loud thuds pounded against a four-inch steel door. "Let me out." The swirling dust on the floor caused Hadassah's eyes to blink several times as she struggled to see more clearly. Her cheek was cold against the concrete that smelled like sweat and urine. The stabbing pain in her neck kept her slightly off kilter as she slowly moved her left hand to her face, rubbing lips so dry they were cracked and painful. She scanned for something familiar and came up empty. A tall, thin girl with an ivory complexion was still screaming, beating and kicking the door, to no avail.

Hadassah's ears perked up at a noise from the other side of the room. Her eyes landed on the parts of the room she could see from her position trying to locate the sound. Her gaze shifted to a young woman nestled in a corner, with her arms wrapped around the knees pulled into her chest. The second girl was brown-skinned and wearing shorts and a blue top, she was sitting on a thin soiled blanket.

Hadassah's mind raced, trying to recreate the movements that landed her here. Why was she on the floor in a strange place, in throbbing pain? She tried to lift her head, but the gripping ache on the right side of her neck signaled that wasn't a good move.

"Wake up everybody, wake up. We have to get out of here." The girl banging on the door had now turned to face the other two people in the room. She was pleading with them through tears coming down so fast, she couldn't possibly see anything. Maybe she wanted them to help her beat against the door, but Hadassah was in no mood to be loud.

"Where are we?" Hadassah asked.

The brown-skinned girl, in the corner, lifted her head to speak. "I've been here for two days now," she replied in a soft, cracking voice. "I don't know where I am or how I got here. Nobody has come to the door or anything."

The girl standing briefly turned to the brown-skinned girl with outstretched hands. "You haven't had nothing to eat or drink?"

"No." she sat up straighter. "I haven't had food or water and I've been using the bathroom in those buckets." She pointed to two five-gallon white paint buckets in one corner.

She rubbed the right side of her neck where Hadassah currently felt a burning ache, "and my neck hurts like hell."

"How long have I been out?" Hadassah mumbled. The girl at the door plopped down suddenly and leaned against the cinderblock wall, extending her legs, and reached for her neck. "I don't have a clue about anything and my neck hurts, too."

The brown girl crawled over to Hadassah and gently shook her. "Hey, you okay? I see your eyes open, but you haven't been moving for a whole day." She stroked a hand across Hadassah's forehead. "I woke up one night, and you were suddenly here." Hadassah was now determined to be stronger than the throbbing she felt in her neck. Even though her body still felt lethargic, her thoughts kicked in as she processed her circumstances and what the others had to say.

The darker girl helped her sit up and the other one moved over to them. They all tried to comfort each other as they searched for signs of something that could provide them with answers. The steel grey door had no knob or lock on the inside. The light above them was dim and provided just enough light for them to make out each other's faces. The room must have been an old storage closet with a few cabinets on the walls, a mop and broom was in one of the corners and the floor was covered with dust. The room smelled of piss and fear.

Hadassah took their hands in hers. "Let's try to think about what happened before we got here."

The girl with the lighter complexion spoke first, "I'm Shayla. All I can remember is last night I threw on these pajama pants and a t-shirt. I went to the corner store to get some pops for me and my grandma. Then I ended up in here." Hadassah turned to her as she was motioning towards a set of Mickey Mouse pajamas. "It's so hard to remember what happened."

She turned to Hadassah, who could finally sit. "I'm Hadassah. Yesterday was my eighteenth birthday. Me and my family was out at the park having a party. I went to the fieldhouse to use the bathroom. I think I remember an old lady being in the bathroom and I asked her if she needed help, but she didn't say anything. On my way out of the bathroom, this guy was by the door and said he was looking for his mother, I turned to walk back in the bathroom and that's the last thing I remember." She was still wearing a pink t-shirt, decorated with the number eighteen in sequins, matching pink leggings and white gym shoes. Hadassah thought of her granny helping her pick out the outfit, saying the color pink would complement her deep ebony skin.

Shayla and Hadassah both turned to the remaining girl.

"Wow, something like that happened to me." She spoke in a heavy whisper. Hadassah wondered where the girl had been, dressed in shorts and a t-shirt with a white logo.

"I was at dance practice and ran to the candy truck to get some water for me and the other girls, then I ended up here. There was a guy behind me telling the lady in the truck to hurry up and move the line so he could go. He was really annoyed; he's the last person I can remember talking.

They all touched their necks within seconds of each other.

"So y'all necks are hurting like mine?" Shayla asked. "You mean to tell me we were snatched in broad daylight and nobody at all tried to help us?"

Then Shayla stood with one hand on her forehead and the other hand on her stomach. Her voice was now raspy.

"So wait, is this like when people be on social media talking about people drugging girls and snatching them off the street and stuff?"

Before Hadassah could respond, Shayla ran to the door, kicking it with all her might. The other girl jumped to her feet and yanked her away. Hadassah could not move because of the drugs she had been given, forcing her to remain in place.

"Hey, be quiet." She warned. "If we have any chance of getting out of here, we can't be making all this noise. There are no windows, no doorknobs, no nothing, so we gotta just wait to see what's going on."

Shayla turned in the other girls' direction. Her tear-stained face and puffy red eyes were a match to how Hadassah felt. "What the hell are you talking about, umm? What's your name?"

"Brittany."

"Well Brittany, in case you haven't figured it out yet, we've been kidnapped and it might be sex trafficking."

She screamed even louder and beat on the door with her fist.

Confusion and fear battled for the lead in Hadassah's mind at hearing Shayla's words, confirming the worst. She struggled to her feet, tried to get her bearings, stepped over to Shayla, leaning against the wall next to the door for support.

"She's right." We don't know what's going on. We're trapped in this room with this dim light, no windows, and no way out." Hadassah rubbed her hands up and down her arms. Although it was summer outside, the room had a damp coolness to it. "Let's be still a minute and try to save our energy in case an opportunity comes. Right now, it looks like we're going to be here until someone comes."

Brittany wrapped her arms around Shayla's shoulder and guided her to sit on one of the dirty blankets spread out against the wall. Hadassah had no more energy left after the brief interaction. She slid to the floor, then had to fight to keep her eyes open, with the pain in her neck now flaring. Now that she was sitting, it was a steady aching throb, still a reminder that someone else was in control.

All three of them flinched when a key turned the lock.

CHAPTER 2

"If you hear from her, please call me." Derek disconnected the call with Carmen,

Hadassah's best friend who wasn't able to attend the birthday party because of her grandmother's funeral. He let out a deep sigh before turning to his mother, who was sitting on the couch gazing expectantly; as though he had answers to how their precious girl could disappear in broad daylight. She ran weathered hands up and down her thighs. The soft material bunching up at her knees.

Unfortunately, he didn't have any good news to share with her. Derek shook his head,

She hasn't talked to her," giving her the sad news that there still had been no contact with

Hadassah. He left the spot by the window, overlooking the bed of tulips, and paced the length of

the living room floor.

"This is not like Hadassah. She wouldn't just go off and not say anything. How could this happen, Derek? Who would do this to us?"

Mama Betty's dark brown eyes watered and the tears spilled down her mahogany cheeks.

Her pain was understandable. Hadassah was a beloved teen with a bright future, despite

being raised by her uncle Derek, grandmother Betty and uncle Louis; mama Betty's youngest

brother. They became her guardians after her parents, Damian and Fatima passed away.

" Let's go through this again." Derek sat in the chair across from this mother.

"Go through what, Derek? You keep asking me the same questions over and over." Mama Betty's voice was an octave below yelling and her fist shook toward his nose, a little too close for comfort.

"I told you I can't remember anything. Why you keep questioning me like I'm a criminal?"

"Because every detail counts. Let's slow down, Mama, take a deep breath."

Mama Betty complied and settled against the sofa, rubbing her palms together. Derek could swear those palms were about to go upside his head.

"You all were in the park, on the East side near Spaulding Street."

"Yes, we were listening to music, eating, some people were dancing, we were just having a good time." She paused, gathering her wits by taking another deep breath. "There were some people having a wedding on the other side."

"Hadassah needed to run to the bathroom. She went to the field house not too far from where we were sitting. That's the last time we saw her."

Derek compared her words to the previous answers, and they were the same.

"When did y'all realize she was missing? How much time had passed?"

"I don't know Derek, I don't know," she said, her grip on the soft material showing her frustration. "Shouldn't you be out looking for clues or something instead of questioning me?"

"Mama, I know this is stressful, but I really need you to think. The first hours when someone goes missing is really important."

Derek moved to perch on the thick wooden cocktail table in front of his mother and reached for her hands.

"Okay, Derek, okay." Mama Betty put her focus on the black angel figurine on the end table across from her. "What if someone has snatched her up? You know, it's a lot of that been going on. People just taking these girls off the street." She shook her head, lacing her hands to stop them from trembling.

"Exactly Mama," he countered. "This is why I need you to think hard. Close your eyes and put yourself back in the park. Even the smallest detail could matter."

Mama Betty shifted on the sofa, then snatched the tissue Derek pulled from the tissue box on the coffee table. "I just need to go home and lay down. All of this is too much."

"You can take a nap in my bedroom," taking her hands back into his. "But I have to ask you a few more questions."

Mama Betty closed her eyes, finding comfort in her son's hands again. "All right, all right, come on."

"Go back to when everybody first made it to the park and started unpacking." She nodded and said, "It was me, Hadassah, Suzette, and Auntie Nell in my car. Tina, ReeRee and the boys were in the car behind mine. Then right on the other side was Belle, Lenora and Lena."

Derek gave her a reassuring squeeze. "Mama, this is so good, look how much you remembered. Keep going." She grimaced and her mouth pressed into a frustrated frown.

"Okay, think Mama, did you see any cars, trucks, anybody that wasn't with the family?"

Her eyes flew open, and she pulled her hands from Derek's and covered her mouth.

"What it is Mama? You remember something?"

Her teary-eyed gaze locked onto his.

"Yes, I do."

CHAPTER 3

The door opened, and the room became tense as they waited for whoever was on the other side. Her heart raced with fear as she would finally come face to face with her captors.

Gold teeth extended to both sides of his mouth. He was tall and muscular with a complexion a hue lighter than ebony. Thick dark sideburns encased his bald head and a long salt and pepper beard divided into three sections with rubber bands covered his chin. His hands were in the pockets of designer jeans.

His gaze shifting between the three girls as he smiled. The younger man with him covered his nose as he said. "Damn, it stinks in here." Shayla jumped to her feet, running at the first man. She clawed at his chest and neck, screaming, "Let me out!" In one vicious motion, he reared back and struck her so hard she flew backwards and landed on the floor, spitting out blood.

"Don't you ever put your hands on me trick," he warned with a raspy growl. "All of you, stand up and let's go."

The girls stood one by one, then gravitated to each other in a comforting huddle.

"Take them to Auntie Nessa's office so she can get a look at our new crew."

The younger man was not much taller than the girls, but walked with the confidence of an NBA player. Life had hardened him, even though he was young and handsome. The black lace-up boots he was wearing didn't make a sound as he moved in front of them. The concrete floor in this new area was the same as the one in the room they had just left, gray from one end to the other. Door after door was a sterile, white steel in the dimly lit, eerily quiet hallway.

A familiar fragrance filled Hadassah's nostrils as they turned the corner. The hallway became colorful, lined with flower pots and rugs on the floor. R&B music filtered from a door that was cracked. Lavender filled her senses as they were each pushed through the doorway by the older man who was following close behind. Hadassah had forgotten his presence while she examined the room. It startled her when he shoved her again.

The woman behind the desk was fanning herself with a large Oriental fan. Hadassah had the strangest recollection of a woman from one of the black and white movies she often watched with her grandmother; Audrey something. The beehive on her head nearly touched the ceiling and the black gloves were tight up to her elbows. Smoke billowed as she puffed hard on a cigarette stuck in a white tip of a long black stick. She graced them with a smile as she came to her feet, standing even taller than the man with the gold teeth. Her thin nose sat perfectly above thick red lips; flawless make-up decorated her impeccable caramel skin. Her beauty and genuine smile made it hard to believe she was on the team of people keeping them in the strange place. Hadassah had to tilt her head to keep watching and listening.

"Welcome," she greeted them and waited for a response. When none came, she said, "No one can find you and how long you will be here depends on you." Her voice was deep and raspy, a heavy Southern drawl, almost like a man's. The woman moved from behind the desk and was now before them, leaning her hips against a massive oak desk. The floor length black dress slightly revealed a pair of muscular legs crossed at her ankles, tipping her ashes in a crystal ashtray. She crossed her arms over a slight bosom and continued to enjoy her cigarette as though she had just welcomed them to a sleep-over. The three girls were still standing close to each other. No one moved. The young man stood to the left of them with his hands in his pockets. The gold teeth man was behind them wearing the same smirk he had in the other room.

Shayla tried to wipe the blood from her mouth and looked up at the woman through a steady stream of tears. Before Shayla could speak, the woman cut her off.

"My name is Auntie Nessa and I'm the 'Keeper'. I keep the girls in line, in order and ready for our customers."

Hadassah tried to keep her expression neutral. "Why did you bring us here? "What did we do to you?" Shayla briefly turned to Hadassah and Brittany as though speaking for all of them before putting her focus back on the woman.

Auntie Nessa placed the cigarette across the ashtray and moved from the desk, while placing her hands on her wide hips. She reached for a tissue from a purple and gold rhinestone studded box and stepped directly in front of Shayla, handing her the thin white sheet. Using one hand, she lifted Shayla's face so that they were eye to eye.

"Boo, it's harsh in this big old world, and everything revolves around money." She took a deep breath as though weary of the conversation. "We are in the business of supply and demand. There is a great demand and you, my pretties, are the supply."

Hadassah and Brittany remained silent as they held onto each other like two people trying to get shelter from the rain under one umbrella. Auntie Nessa held Shayla's face for a moment longer, examining her bruised lip and the purple color forming on her cheek in the form of a handprint.

She turned, glaring at the man with the gold teeth. "Benny T, what happened to her face? I told you about that quick temper of yours. These men don't want to pay for damaged merchandise."

Benny T sucked his teeth and, for a moment, looked like he wanted to spit on the floor.

"Man, look, you know we gotta keep these hoes in order," he snapped. "If one of them gets out of line, they might all try it." He smirked as his gaze flickered between Auntie Nessa and the girls. "You know what to do to fix her up. Put one of them concoctions together you be making."

"You can leave now," she said with a warning look at him before focusing on the younger man. "Van, go get the holding room cleaned up. Benny T, step outside and close the door."

Nessa finally turned her attention back to the girls and said, "I need all three of you to take a seat on the couch." Hadassah watched the others out of the corner of her eye. Like her, they seemed afraid to move.

"It's okay, Shugas. This is a rough situation and Auntie Nessa not gon' cut any corners with you. I'm going to give it to you straight with no chaser." She motioned again for them to move towards the lush purple couch. "Come on now, let's dry all these tears, and sit down so I can tell you what has happened."

She sat in the purple chair kitty corner to the couch. After re-lighting the cigarette at the end of her smoking stick, she lifted the floor length dress up to her knees and gracefully crossed one leg over the other.

"This is the beginning of the most fu-, wait," she grimaced. "He doesn't like us to use profanity." Shayla turned to the door and back to Auntie Nessa. No one else had come in.

"Oh pardon me dear," Auntie Nessa touched the strand of pearls about her neck. "The *he* is your new boss, who you will meet soon."

"What do you mean, our new boss?" Brittany slid to the edge of the couch, hands on her knees. "What are you talking about? I don't have a job or a boss."

Auntie Nessa took a long sigh and tipped the ashes. "I'm trying not to get all ugly here." She said through her teeth. "Please don't interrupt me when I'm speaking." Brittany frowned and slid back.

"Ya'll can make this as hard as you want to," she warned. "You are all now employed in this here establishment."

"Employed doing what?" Hadassah asked, afraid to move and equally afraid of the answer.

"Now that's the question you should all be asking." Her smile struck a chord of fear in Hadassah's heart. "But you know what? We'll answer that another time." She suddenly stopped. "Let me go ahead and answer that now. You have been kidnapped from wherever you were and you now work as escorts for the Bayou." She paused, but wasn't really waiting for a response. "I need to show you all where you'll be sleeping for a while. Get up, let's go. Benny T." she yelled towards the door.

Brittany jumped to her feet. "Wait, wait a minute," she cried, holding her hands out to touch Auntie Nessa. "You don't have to do this. You don't have to keep us here. My family has money, my father is a doctor and my mother is a nurse. They can pay you."

Benny T rushed into the room and pushed Brittany to the couch.

"Ain't nobody going nowhere. Like Auntie Nessa just said. Y'all employees now. How long you will work here is up to you." He shook a finger at Brittany. "Don't move unless you're told to move. Don't speak unless you're told to speak. Now, we're going to try this again. Let's go."

The girls stood and huddled against each other again.

Benny walked to the door and motioned for them to follow. Brittany, Hadassah and Shayla all looked to Auntie Nessa first.

"Gone head now, it's gon' be okay," her face forming a sour expression. "Don't go making Benny mad, we don't want no more busted lips and bruised up faces."

"You ain't gotta keep talking and pacifying these tricks," he shot back. "They need to get used to this new lifestyle. They some tricks and they gone be tricking with some tricks." He laughed at his own play on words.

Auntie Nessa shook her head, evidently unable to appreciate his humor. "Now stop all this whining and crying. I said let's go." This time, they all followed without saying a word.

CHAPTER 4

*H*adassah awakened to the sun struggling to find its place in the small room. She tried to clear the grogginess from her mind and recall the past night after she and the other girls were served a delicious meal. She was just as puzzled by these surroundings as she had been waking up in the holding room. Even more puzzling was her being dressed in a hospital gown, covered by a thin white sheet and a sticky substance was on the inside of her thighs.

On one side, Shayla was still asleep, on the other side Brittany was staring at the ceiling, unmistakable tears pooling on the pillow. A hospital gown covered her body as well.

The bars on the windows were a rusted brown. Hadassah raised up slowly to her elbows, processing the scene with the three people who had made themselves known yesterday.

Just as the thoughts were falling into place, Auntie Nessa walked in. "Wake up, honeys, let's wake up." The Keeper of the girls was now dressed in a black jumpsuit that snugged her body, with about ten strands of pearls that draped to her belly. Her red beret covered a black bobbed wig, her make-up as flawless as the day before. Hadassah recognized the Egyptian musk oil as the same scent her uncle Derek wore. She wondered if he was searching for her and silently prayed that he was.

The woman sashayed to an old wooden desk against the opposite wall and lit a cigarette.

"So, it seems, ladies, that Brittany and you Hadassah are still virgins and will fetch a higher price, but you, Ms. Shayla have been quite the busy one already."

All three girls shared a questioning glance. Hadassah reached down to the sticky substance between her legs. The realization set in that they had been drugged, violated, and an examination had been performed on each of them while they slept.

"Y'all is some freaks", Shayla screamed, still coming out of her slumber. "What did ya'll do to us? Why are we naked? Y'all been feeling between our legs while we was sleep? Y'all drugged us with that food last night."

She was now up, walking towards Auntie Nessa. The gray steel door opened suddenly and Benny T stepped in. "Get back on that bed trick." His eyes met Shayla's with an icy stare. Auntie Nessa flicked the ashes from her cigarette, unbothered by Shayla's aggression. "Everybody just calm down."

Hadassah was hoping she complied quickly before Benny T took another swing and added more bruises to the previous ones.

"Everything's okay Benny T. You can relax. And I wish you would stop calling the girls tricks."

"Like I said, they some tricks and gon' be living that trick life." He put his focus on Shayla who quickly backed up to the bed, pulled the yellow sheet up to her face, sobbing. "Let's begin now that we have everyone's attention."

"What do you mean, higher price? Are you trying to sell us?" Brittany asked.

"Listen, we done told ya'll what it is." Benny T yelled; frustration in every word. "Y'all gon' make us money for as long as we say and y'all gone use y'all young tight pus-" Auntie Nessa cut in, giving him a hard look. "No profanity Benny."

"Right, Right" he said with a chuckle while throwing his hand up in mock surrender.

Auntie Nessa sighed, and the sound caused Benny T's laughter to cut off. "Ol' Auntie Nessa, trying to be all diplomatic. This is what it is. Y'all can make this new situation hard or easy. All of you was gone end up giving that cookie away for free anyway. At least here you'll have food and shelter." She grinned. "Let's say, an exchange of sorts."

Two days ago she was celebrating her eighteenth birthday, now she was being held prisoner by people who had plans to sell her body. The only hope she had was to pray like her grandmother had taught her; prayers that somehow, she would come out of this situation alive.

Now let's all get cleaned up and put on some clothes you so you can meet the other girls.

Other girls? There's more of us?

They gave each girl a warm towel to wipe the sticky substance from between their legs and a smaller one for their faces. A pair of jeans, a white t-shirt and a pair of gym shoes were on the small stands at the end of each bed. Benny T led them down a dark hallway with many doors until they came to a pair of red double doors that looked like they were from a plantation-style house in a movie.

Hadassah's jaw went slack as she scanned the room. The girls sitting around on red and black velvet sofas and chairs represented every ethnicity. They glowed as though they were runway models. Their make-up looked professionally done and their arms and legs were shiny and smooth. All of them were drinking water or some type of juice and eating small plates of fruit and vegetables and other healthy things.

"Get over there and sit down." Benny T commanded with his arm extended towards an empty sofa near a spread of food.

Auntie Nessa stepped into the room with a lit cigarette in one hand and a full glass of amber liquid in the other.

"Bayou Beauties, meet the newbies. Newbies, these are the Beauties of the Bayou." The girls waved or nodded, none of them said a word.

Hadassah tried to contain her confusion. *"Are these girls' prisoners* too?" The smiles on their faces and postures of their bodies didn't read prisoner at all. In fact, they all looked quite comfortable and settled, as if they were at home. That frightened her more than anything she'd encountered so far. They had accepted what had happened to them. She never would.

CHAPTER 5

"Here Here." All five people stood and raised their glasses. "Let's raise a toast to our newly re-elected President. Viktor Batista." The four people in the room obliged.

"Thank you, thank you, thank you to each one of you for your continued support. I wanted to celebrate you all privately, away from the public eye. Benny T, no one keeps us covered the way you do."

Viktor handed his head of security an envelope that he immediately stuffed in his pocket with a big gold-toothed grin.

"Bill, your management of our campaign funds keeps everyone off our case and out of our business." He handed him the same-colored envelope as he did Benny T. Bill tilted the envelope towards Viktor in a nod of thanks before tucking it inside his suit jacket.

"The Towers are in the best shape ever and sure to garner us some additional grants and funding in this coming year." He pushed an envelope across the table to Mr. Lattimore, the head of Building Management.

"And finally, to you Auntie Nessa," he said, giving her a healthy once-over. "You keep me healthy mentally, spiritually and physically and you take care of the Towers' most precious possession–the Bayou Beauties."

Auntie Nessa reached for a silver switchblade, placing it on top of the envelope he handed her and gracefully placed both items in her bra; smiling before taking another sip of the dark liquor in her snifter.

"Now everyone, I have a surprise for you." He gestured to the sofa across from him. "Take a seat, please."

They settled on the two-piece luxurious soft gray sectional. "Auntie Nessa, we're ready when you are."

She primped her oversized beehive wig. "Viktor, there was a slight problem with our *surprise* today." Viktor frowned and the others tensed. "What type of problem?" He swept a gaze over the others, who shifted uncomfortably and remained silent. "Why didn't I know about it before now?"

Nessa scooted to the edge of the sofa.

"I didn't want to bother you with this. Cheyenne got her cycle this morning, so she won't be able to perform this evening."

Viktor sat his drink on the glass end table separating the sectionals. He placed his palms slightly apart and tapped his fingertips on the top knee of his crossed legs.

"So, I hope this means you selected another beauty for the job tonight."

Auntie Nessa lowered her gaze to her freshly manicured hands.

"Yes, I think you'll li-"

"Never mind," he snapped. "Bring in Cecelia. She's a favorite of everyone here. Go and fetch her, please." Auntie Nessa's anxious look belied the calm she radiated. Her gaze landed on Benny T who was grinning and making himself comfortable.

"Yeah, go ahead and get Ms. Cecelia," he taunted. "We haven't seen that as-. I mean, we haven't seen her dance in years."

Auntie Nessa sashayed to the door, but her heart was heavy. One thing Viktor hated the most was to be kept waiting. But he had also made a promise and was breaking it. Within minutes, she returned with Cecelia. A green-eyed woman with olive skin, a slender, curvy build. Her backside and breast were still firm and toned from her days as an athlete. Three years ago, Cecelia Tradeau got promoted to

Queen Beauty, which removed her from the list for private dancing that Vik is now demanding.

Cecilia scanned the faces of the people in Vik's office and her facial expression went from pleasant to questioning. "Yes, Viktor," she said in a sultry voice. "Did you need something?"

As she had been taught years before, she crossed her hands in front of her submissively. Viktor rose to his full height, towering over her. He moved close and gently stroked his fingers through her long, dark brown hair, before slightly gripping it. He looked directly into her green eyes.

"Yes, my dear, I do want something." His creole accent was thicker any time he was annoyed, and that struck a note of fear in Auntie Nessa's mind. "I would like for you to perform for me and my guests tonight." Cecilia's body tensed as she struggled to glance over her shoulder and found that all eyes were on her. She tried to take a step back, but Viktor moved in and tightened his grip enough that her head snapped back.

"I thought I no longer had to work the rooms or do private parties." She whispered, her gaze now focused towards the floor and her cheeks flushed a crimson color.

He spoke with a calculated intensity. "That is what I said, at that time." He took a deep breath, moving her head so she was looking into his eyes again.

She winced, and a whimper of pain escaped her throat.

"And now I'm saying I want you to dance for us. Is this going to be a problem?"

Benny T sat up, tapping his knees with clenched fists. The tension in the room ramped up. Someone sighed their impatience; Auntie Nessa couldn't tell who.

"Viktor this is not fair," she whined in a shaky voice. "You have me running errands, going to buy food and getting the girls' clothes now. There are twenty other girls. Why can't it be one of them?"

Viktor inhaled and his shoulders flexed as though it took every ounce of strength to remain calm. He twisted the lock of hair in his hand, jerking her head a little. "My dear Cecelia, you know I don't ask anything twice, but I'm feeling a bit festive today. I said I want you to dance to celebrate my victory."

"Viktor please," she cried, tears streaming down her face. "You haven't let anyone see me for three years now, three years and you wa-."

Viktor pushed her hard, freeing her hair from his hold, before returning to his desk. He nodded to Benny T, who understood the instruction to remove Cecelia from their establishment. "Her services are no longer needed."

Her eyes widened with terror. She held up hands as Benny T moved towards her, grinning as though he had won the lottery.

"No, wait, okay," she protested, inching backwards. "I'll do it, I'll do it," reaching for the top buttons of her blouse.

She hadn't made it to the third button when Benny T grabbed her arm and yanked her towards the door. Bill, Auntie Nessa, and Mr. Lattimore remained motionless.

"Please Benny T, no, I'll do it, I'll dance."

"Too late for that now, trick. Let's go." In one motion, Benny T grabbed Cecelia around her waist, picked her up and carried her out screaming Viktor's name.

Viktor smoothed his tie, cleared his throat before he looked at the people in the room, and smiled. With a nod, he reclaimed his seat before he spoke as though nothing out of the ordinary had happened. "It appears that I have to extend an IOU on the private dance. I'll be in touch soon."

Viktor Batista was a man of few words, so there was nothing else that needed to be said. Everyone stood, said their goodbyes and rushed to make a hasty exit.

"Auntie Nessa can I speak with you a moment, please?"

She froze as she braced herself and tipped back to the sofa.

"Now that I have to dispose of Cecelia," he said, face tight with anger. "Who do you think is ready to step up and take on the role of Bayou leader?"

Auntie Nessa was struggling to hold back tears.

"You could've given her another chance. I mean, you did spring it on her at the last minute to just come in here and start dancing in front of some of her old customers." She pulled a pack of cigarettes from her bra and lit one as she spoke, measuring her words.

"Auntie Nessa, I run these whores or, as Benny calls them, *tricks.*" He grinned, "and I have been doing so for the last ten years. They do what I say, when I say, how I say. She defied me in front of our guests. Now you know that was unacceptable. Look at all she has now since I promoted her." He waved a slow open palm in her direction. "Who does she think she is to defy me? "My mother would never do such a thing to my father."

Auntie Nessa sat back in the chair until it reached her comfort with a deep exhale.

"What do you mean your mother would never do this to your father? They've been married for over twenty-five years. Aren't they partners in the business at this point?" She chided. She knew anytime Vik mentioned his parents, he was going to tell the story of how they met and how the Batista pimping legacy began.

"My mother Collette was living in a run-down trailer park, barely surviving when she met my father." He smiled as he laid his head against the soft leather of his wide backed chair.

"You don't say." Auntie Nessa quipped with pretended curiosity. She had heard the story many times, but knew better than to say so.

"A trick was getting rough with her one night to the point of her having to fight to get away. She ran into the truck stop and sat down right next to my father and whispered, 'please help me.'

"My father didn't know what was going on, but being the southern gentleman that he still is today, he said okay." When the trick came busting through the door, Big Vik offered my mother a bite of his sandwich to signal she was not alone. The trick left. My mother taught my father the game, and that's where the Batista empire began." He spoke as though he was telling a child a bed-time story. Auntie Nessa let him sit with his nostalgia a moment before she spoke.

"Okay, Viktor," she said through a puff of smoke. "Cecelia's gone, you never go back on your word, so what's next, or should I say, *who* is next?" He grabbed the files that were in the envelope from Mrs. Wilkerson from the metal basket on his desk.

After opening the second file, he raised his eyebrows and leaned against the back of the chair. "Hadassah?"

CHAPTER 6

The tall, muscular woman took up the full space of the door as she flickered a gaze over the ones in front of her. "Okay, newbies. You've seen the girls, now its time to meet your new boss, so we are all properly introduced."

Brittany stood first, slowly walking over to Auntie Nessa in a robotic walk that spoke of her shocked status.

"Why are you all doing this? Why did you pick us? Isn't this illegal?"

Her hands were in a tight prayer position as she glanced over at the other two girls. "I swear to God if you let me go, I won't tell nobody what happened. Please, let me go. I'm sixteen years old. My parents have money. This can't be happening." She tried to reach Auntie Nessa's hands. "Please let me go."

Before Auntie Nessa could respond, Benny T gave her a hard nudge from behind, then moved so he was directly in Brittany's face.

"Ya'll about to piss me off," he snarled. "Don't speak unless you're told to."

He pushed her close to Shayla and Hadassah, almost knocking them over.

"Yes, you been snatched up," he roared. "Yes, we're going to sell your ass. No, we ain't letting you go. No, no one can find you. Yes, you are now our property." His voice was one tone below yelling, but still effective. All three girls were now huddled together.

"And all this crying is about to piss me off even more," he snapped. "Now shut it up."

Auntie Nessa gave each girl a thin face towel from the stack next to the sheets and gowns.

"Dry your faces," she commanded. "It's time to meet the owner of our fine establishment. He doesn't like a lot of talking and don't interrupt while he's speaking. If you do, you'll have to deal with ol' Benny T here." She pointed in his direction and his face split into an irritating grin.

They complied before following Auntie Nessa down a different hallway, until they reached two big oak doors, that seemed just as out of place as they red ones where they met the other girls.

Auntie Nessa stepped into the office first and motioned the girls in.

A man in a designer suit moved from behind the desk and leaned against the front edge. He gave them a charming smile and opened his arms the full width of their measure and said with a deep accent that Hadassah couldn't place, "Ladies, welcome to the Bayou. You, my lovelies, are now Bayou Beauties." He hands lowered to his side and she took in the fact that his nails were manicured.

"Twenty of the most in demand: beautiful and expensive escorts, or *fille de joies.*"

His words resembled a man from another old show Hadassah watched with her grandmother. Every week, the man welcomed everyone to an island. Only, this was no island or fantasy, more of a nightmare from which she had not awakened.

"Please, ladies." He gestured to a place behind them. Have a seat and let's get to know each other."

The girls sat close to each other on the grey suede sofa.

He claimed a spot in front of them, with a drink in a crystal glass.

"I would like to know your name and what side of the city you're from."

No one moved or spoke. The room was pin-drop quiet. "I under-stand your hesitation. Let's start with you," he said, focusing on Brittany. "You're the one from a little money, so there will definitely be someone looking for you."

She shifted a puzzled glance to Auntie Nessa, who grimaced, but didn't give any direction.

"I only ask once. Let's not start off on a bad note." The dark glint in his eyes didn't match the charm in the thick accented voice. Hadassah nudged Brittany, who said, "I'm Brittany from the southeast side."

"Nice to meet you, Brittany."

He nodded turning to face Shayla. "And you are?"

She shifted, gripping Hadassah's hand next to her thighs. "I'm Shayla," and I'm from the Hundreds."

"Ah yes, Ms. Shayla, due to what we learned from your examination, you'll be in a room with one of our more experienced girls." His smile struck a chord of fear in Hadassah's heart. She felt anxious for this girl. "Your clientele' will be slightly different."

Shayla opened her mouth to protest, but clamped down on anything she had to say.

"And you, what's your name?"

"Hadassah." Viktor gave her a long look and a slight smile that held no warmth. "Is it really? Growing up in the bible belt, I'm familiar with that name being from the book of Esther." He leaned forward. "And who gave you that name, may I ask?"

"My father." Hadassah tried to be brave and look Viktor in his eyes, but the steadiness of his gaze and the darkness of those eyes were unnerving. He leaned back in the chair and crossed his legs.

"And who, may I ask, gave you such deep melanated skin?"

"My mother," she replied softly as a pang of loneliness overcame her. She had been gifted only a few years with her mother and father, who died when she was just nine years old.

"Dark, yet she is lovely," he mused quoting scripture, his voice holding a note of something that made Hadassah shudder. "I can foresee this one being in high demand once you have that skin shining and glowing, Nessa."

Auntie Nessa nodded, and her gaze raked over Hadassah dismissively.

"Well, ladies. I just wanted to see you for myself so you can know who I am, and who you will be working for from this point on."

He stood, gave them a parting look and, without another word, left the office.

The girls sat quietly for a moment before they looked to Auntie Nessa, who put out her cigarette.

"Let's get you assigned to your roommates and begin your routines."

"Roommates, routines. We're going to be here that long?" Shayla screeched before a sob echoed down the hallway.

Hadassah stroked her back and whispered. "Calm down. Let's not make Benny T put his hands on you again."

CHAPTER 7

"There was a truck. A big black truck, it was real clean and shiny." Mama Betty was now standing. She moved into the open area next to the cocktail table where Derek was sitting. She rubbed her temples as though a headache was coming on. "It had some funny-looking plates. Hadassah went back to the car to get another chair. She said something to the man that was leaning against the truck. I joked with her and asked if he was dropping off one of her friends from her fancy school."

Derek scribbled that information on a small pad.

"Think, Mama, what was it about the truck that made you say that?"

Mama Betty paused, hands trembling with the effort to access her memory bank.

"The plates, it was some of those plates, like the ones I've seen when I stopped by the police station with you a couple of times."

Derek took out his phone and scrolled to an image. "You mean something like this?" he moved so she could peer at the screen.

"Almost, something like that." She pressed her finger and thumb together and zoomed in.

"This is it. Something real close to this." Derek took a screenshot of the plates that were city officials and then tucked the phone back into his pocket.

"Keep going Mama, what else?"

"The man said something to Hadassah, and she spoke back. She got the chair and came to sit with us and that was it."

"Wait Mama, did the man by the truck come over to Hadassah, or did he just speak?" Mama Betty's hands clasped on her lap after sitting back down. "Let me think, let me think."

She held up her hand and lowered them again, giving Derek the signal to hold on a moment. "When Hadassah was walking back with the chair, the truck pulled off. I told Hadassah, 'I guess those weren't some of your fancy friends.' We laughed and started setting up. I didn't see the truck again."

"The party started and everyone was dancing, laughing and talking. Hours later, we noticed Hadassah was missing."

Derek stepped in to embrace his mother. "Mama, this is going to help so much. I gotta run to the station."

"You just gonna leave me and your auntie here?"

"Yes, Mama." Derek had gathered the rest of his things and dropped them into a small duffle bag. "If anyone calls the landline, you'll be here to answer it."

"What are you gonna do at the station?"

Derek tried not to be frustrated with this mother and all her questions because he understood it all came from fear and worry; but every minute of inquiry delayed his investigation.

He came over to her side and gently touched her arms. "Mama, these look like government plates," he replied. "I'm going to the station to check into it. If you and Auntie leave, make sure you turn on the answering machine and turn on the alarm."

Mama Betty sighed and held onto him for a moment. "Okay, baby, go head." She ambled towards the stairs; her bearing was as though she carried the weight of her fear on her shoulders.

Derek didn't have that luxury. He had to find his niece before she was lost to them forever.

CHAPTER 8

The first few nights had given the girls a small window to talk and get to know each other. The system had taken Shayla from her drug addicted mother and placed her with her grandmother who fought for six months to take custody. She didn't have the same luck with Shayla's two younger sisters. She was already familiar with the world of sex trafficking; her mother had been pimping her to support her habit for a year before someone dropped a dime and the state stepped in. Now at seventeen, fighting and fending for herself was her norm.

Brittany's home life compared in deep contrast. Growing up with successful parents had her in a never-ending cycle of over achieving. This led to her cutting herself and needing meds to cope with her mental state.

Every day, they had an introduction to something new about their environment.

The first thing Hadassah noticed in the enormous kitchen were the pungent smells; strong and earthy.

She had never seen so many jars of oils and herbs in one place. They had converted two apartments to what looked like a gourmet kitchen. There was every kind of herb and plant, and a wall-sized medicine cabinet filled with jars and bottles with several plant mixtures. One entire wall was cabinets of various sizes. On the far left, a mini-greenhouse was in operation.

The kitchen was complete with two large stainless-steel refrigerators and a huge deep freezer like the one in her grandmother's house. The window had limited sunlight coming in because it blocked some parts of it off, making it too small for a body to fit through.

She couldn't believe a setup like this was part of their captivity.

"All right ladies, take a seat." Auntie Nessa wore an apron and donned a head wrap to cover that signature hairstyle. The girls sat in chairs next to each other.

She went past the dishwasher and stood next to the wall that held jars filled with liquids, gels, plants, and herbs. There was so much to look at, it felt almost mystical. She moved her hand along the items, gently touching the jars as she spoke. "This is where the magic begins. I handcraft all of your oils, lotions, potions, baths, shampoos and moisturizers for your skin and hair."

"What's all this for?" Hadassah asked, following the woman's movements.

"Baby, this is for your dates."

"What do you mean, dates?" Brittany put a grip on Shayla's hand to stop her from trembling too.

Auntie Nessa parted her mouth to speak, but stopped and smiled. "We'll get to that."

The girls shared an anxious glance, then focused on Nessa again.

She walked to the other side of the room where the stove and refrigerator were. "I also prepare all the food. Your diet from here on out is fruits, vegetables, beans, nuts, whole grains, juices, water, and nut milks."

"No meat?" Hadassah questioned. "No fish or chicken?"

"What? You kidnap us and turn us into vegans. This is some bull," Shayla screamed. She slouched back in the chair, crossing her arms. Hadassah's gaze shifted to the door to see if Benny T would walk in.

"Ms. Shayla, mind your words, l'il girl. I keep telling you this situation is what it is. As I told you on your first day here, it's going to be what *you* make it."

Shayla huffed and rolled her eyes.

"As I was saying. I prepare all the meals for the girls, Mr. Batista, and the staff. You'll eat three meals a day and no one eats after seven unless you have a late date." She raised an eyebrow as Hadassah released a breath she didn't realize she was holding.

"As part of your regiment, you'll work out three times a week by walking the stairs and strength training." Auntie Nessa lit a cigarette and leaned against the stove as she spoke. "Once a month, you will go outside to breathe and get some fresh air." Hadassah kept trying to process what was really happening, but none of it made sense.

Brittany raised her hand.

"Yes baby, what is it?"

Brittany turned to Nessa with eyes so filled with tears it was probably impossible to see. "When is somebody going to explain exactly what we're going to be doing? You're sitting here talking to us like this is a resort or something." She glanced at the other two girls for support, but they remained silent. "We're gonna be working out, eating like vegetarians or something and using specials oils and lotions." She leaned forward in the chair. "Y'all took us and now y'all wanna act like we in some specialized training for some executive level jobs." She turned to Shayla and Hadassah. "Are y'all hearing this?"

Both girls looked at each other, then the door before speaking. "She already told me to shut up, so I ain't got nothing to say, other than this is a fu-, I mean a messed-up situation and we're stuck here," Shayla huffed.

Auntie Nessa glanced at her with a disdainful air before placing the tip back in her red mouth. "Since you all have questions, let's just get to it." She moved to the chair at the head of the table. They complied. The silence from the other parts of the house was uncanny. They met seventeen other girls last night. *What was everyone else doing?*

"This place that you are now a part of is called the Bayou, as Mr. Batista told you."

"Why is it called the Bayou if we're not by any water?" Shayla questioned with raised hands and shoulders.

Nessa snatched her holder out of her mouth, glaring at Shayla.

"Oh sorry, for interrupting you. I thought you said if we have questions." Shayla looked at the door and then back to Auntie Nessa, with one look, she now understood the drill.

Nessa took her time before speaking again. "I don't want to have to send any of you to Benny T for any reminders; like interrupting me. It will not be a pleasant experience." She let them absorb that for a moment.

"As I was saying. You are in the Bayou. There are twenty girls including you. We sell sex, but more than that, we sell fantasy." She gave each girl a steely look. "There are seven rooms your date has to choose from. The movie and chill room, naughty school girl, naughty nurse, freaky teacher, night out on the town, BDSM, and freaky-neeky room."

The girls shifted a little, but had the common sense not to ask the burning question the last words brought to mind.

"Every time you have a date, it costs the gentlemen one thousand for one hour."

Hadassah hadn't seen that much money at one time ever. McDonald's paid fifteen dollars an hour. This time the girls looked at each other with wide-eyed amazement. She couldn't wrap her head around what would happen in a room with a man for one thousand dollars.

"Since you are new, you won't be having any dates for thirty days."

Hadassah raised her hand to speak. "Yes, Ms. Dark and Lovely."

"What are we going to be doing for thirty days?"

"Now that's a great question my dear. You will be drinking detox teas, eating alkaline foods, working out and getting your young bodies prepared. Viktor prides himself on having the highest quality brothel known in these parts."

Hadassah raised her hand again, but didn't wait for the queue to speak. "What are these parts? Are we still in the city?"

Auntie Nessa took a long pull from her cigarette. "That, my dear is *not* for you to know."

Brittany nudged Hadassah into silence.

"You've been here for four days now," she informed them. Hadassah made a mental note to keep track of the days from this point on, using the sunlight from the kitchen window to keep track of sunrise and sunset.

"Over the next thirty days, I'll be trying essentials oils, lotions and body butters on your skin. I'm going to get your hair in order and assign you a new name."

With each passing moment, Hadassah's hope sank. Without a doubt she knew her family was searching for her.

"You'll also be in training for how to behave on a date; what to say and what not to say." Hadassah folded her hands and dropped them in her lap in quiet disbelief. How did her entire world change in one day? A few days ago she was at the park celebrating her entrance into adulthood birthday and now she was part of some underground brothel.

She tried to recall every conversation she had with Uncle Derek of what to do if she ever got caught up in a situation like this.

Pay attention to every detail. Let no one know who you are under any circumstances because they could use your family to keep you in line.

Uncle Derek had taught her to listen to every name and keep track of the time. Four days in, time was ticking. These people had blocked off every avenue of escape. Windows had been blocked or barred. The hallways were a maze of doors. She couldn't remember her way back to her room because they seem to travel a different way each time. Was everyone blocked off from outside contact? How could she get any type of message to her family? Especially since Auntie Nessa had said they would only see sunlight for short periods of time.

Another hand raise from Shayla interrupted Hadassah's thoughts.

"Yes, honey," Auntie Nessa said with a weary sigh. "You have another question for Auntie?'

Hadassah put a warning grip on Shayla's knee.

"Yes, I do." Shayla leaned inward with a steely glaze on Auntie Nessa that signaled mischief. "I've been wanting to ask you this since the first day we met you."

Auntie Nessa puffed her cigarette and draped one arm over the back of her chair

"Gon' head honey what's on your mind?"

"Are you really a man?"

CHAPTER 9

"Listen DC, we gotta make this real quick," Malik said in a solemn tone. "You know I can't get caught having no conversations with 5-0."

The man with golden skin was wearing a hoodie and a pair of expensive gym shoes, pulled his hood down and kept his face low as the vehicle turned the corner into a dark alley.

"Man I get it. I'll be brief. I'm just trying to find my niece." Derek said leaning towards Malik, tapping his steering wheel. "I believe she's been snatched up like these other girls in the city. Crazy thing is though my Mama saw a big clean truck in the park, right before my niece went missing. The truck had some kind of special plates."

The young man froze with his hand halfway to his face. His gaze darted about, landing everywhere except on Derek.

Derek didn't know what he said to cause such a reaction from his young informant.

"What's wrong with you? You look like you just saw a ghost."

Malik grimaced as he focused on the green dumpster to the left of the vehicle, weighing his thoughts. He'd provided intel that had closed so many cases that the brass thought Derek had a magic wand. The secret was always money. He paid Malik more than the standard CI rates, with that extra cost coming out of his own pocket. But it was worth it to solve crimes that the other detectives pushed to the side especially if it involved people of color.

"DC, do you know who that is?"

Malik's tawny skin was almost flush with heat as he replied.

"Naw man. Who are you talking about? What's up?"

Malik forgot he was supposed to be hiding out and sat up to be level with Derek.

"Man, everyone knows that Vik B is snatching girls up in the big Escalade and nobody can touch him because he's connected."

Derek's heart slammed in his chest. Finally; a concrete lead.

"Connected to who? Who is Vik B?" Derek questioned.

"Look I can't be doing too much talking," Malik replied with a shrug "But check it. Word in the underground is Vik B has one of the hottest spots out West, with the prettiest girls, that'll do the wildest things. A grip for sixty minutes. But dude is so plugged can't nobody get to him; not even you. And he takes referrals, from trusted people only." He scanned their location. "Aye, drop me two blocks over, I gotta ride."

"That's love B." He handed Malik a crispy hundred-dollar bill and pulled off.

Derek Colton, known on the street at "DC", had risen to detective status within eighteen months of being on the force. His street cred gave him a golden ticket and opportunities to gain intel that other officers weren't able to gain at gun point. Along with gaining a new title, he also gained lots of enemies, within the force and on the street. He was one of the few officers who worked in Chicago with a level of integrity; unlike some cops who hid behind that blue wall of silence and remained on the force long past their expiration date.

On a personal level, he had become the stand-in father to his niece Hadassah after a crash on the Eisenhower expressway killed her father, his older brother Damian along with his wife Fatima during a winter pile-up. Raised on the Westside in the area known as the Holy

City, he was no stranger to the world of sex trafficking and guerilla pimping.

Most times he solved those cases on a quest to find a murderer or drug lord which it appears his niece had fallen victim to.

The fact that he could not keep his niece from becoming prey weighed on him. He couldn't even elicit the help of his fellow boys in blue.

Before pulling away from the stop sign, he prayed that everything he had poured into her would help. He used to take her to different stores and restaurants to teach her how to survey a situation, check for exits and lock the details in her memory.

Always count the number of people and weapons if you see any.

Keeping track of time was vital. And she should never give in to a victim mindset. Play the game she needed to play to come out on top. He hoped that all the Tae-Kwan-Do classes she had taken would be useful as well.

Finding out everything there was to know about Vik B and how he was politically connected would take some finessing. Chicago was saddled in dirty politics and even dirtier politicians. He was on his own for the moment. His partner, Richard Meeks known on the streets as Richie Rich, was lying in a hospital bed on a ventilator fighting for his life. The man had taken down the worse criminals involved in missing girls, drugs, money laundering and gun running; but he'd lost a battle against an enemy he never saw coming, COVID-19. He was sure Vik B had some CPD officers on his payroll for him to be in business for any length of time. Being a detective with few allies made the path for getting information that much harder.

He had to find out if this Vik B had actually snatched Hadassah up, so he could move on if he found out he should be looking elsewhere. His gut was telling him he was on the right track. He had to go with it, he couldn't waste any time, just in case somebody else had snatched her up.

He tapped a clenched fist against his lips until the dread-locked brother behind him in a souped-up Charger, honked, causing Derek to look up and see the man's expression; with a look of '*what are you going to do?*'

Derek could hear a Tupac song filtering in from the charger.

"I love my Mama too brother."

He threw up a power fist and moved through the intersection.

CHAPTER 10

$\mathcal{A}$ long-legged girl with shiny pecan-colored skin, laid the magazine on her flat stomach and focused on Auntie Nessa and Hadassah the moment the door opened.

Hadassah's new roommate was young, but the lines around her eyes said she had seen some better days. She would be sure to ask how long she had been at the Bayou when they were alone.

"Sam meet Hadassah. Hadassah you'll be hanging out with Samantha, who goes by Sam."

Sam raised a limp palm in Hadassah's direction and picked up the magazine, so the full spread covered her face.

The room was just big enough for two small dressers at the end of two twin beds. All the walls were a soft yellow. and the floor, a gray tile with white and yellow specks.

"She ain't the most friendly," Aunt Nessa quipped, "but she came here a virgin,

same as you. She's one of our most in demand, so she she'll teach you the ropes."

Sam chuckled from behind the pages and the sound chilled Hadassah's soul. It conveyed much in that moment that Hadassah realized her efforts at escape might be harder than she imagined. "Yes ma'am, Sam has 'em going crazy for her, buying her jewelry and presents."

Sam spoke from behind the magazine, "gifts and presents that I can't wear nowhere but with other tricks." Those words sent a deeper chill down Hadassah's spine.

"I'll let you two get to know each other while I place the other girls. Dinner is at five, and you don't want to be late," she warned with a finger wagging at her. "Mr. B is joining us tonight."

Sam sat up and placed the magazine over her crossed ankles. She put a dark glare on Auntie Nessa. "So, I heard they have *disposed of Cecelia* and Mr. B is looking for a new head Beauty."

Something about the word disposed did not sit well with Hadassah. Fired. Let go maybe. Disposed of sounded more ominous, and if Benny T was involved it was. "And how did you hear all of that Ms. Sam?" Auntie Nessa was leaning against the door frame with one hand on her hip and a lit cigarette in the other, but there was no mistaking her anger. "I done told you more than once about repeating things you hear. Gossiping is a sin."

Sam snatched up the magazine and returned to the original position on the bed with the book blocking her face. "Gurl please, don't start with all that church stuff you be talking. Y'all got us in here selling ass out of every drawer hole and you wanna talk about gossiping being a sin."

"Watch the profanity, Ms. Sam." Nessa stood tall and flicked the ashes in the pocket of her apron. The move shocked Hadassah who expected the woman to have a crystal ashtray in every room.

"Yeah, I know, Mr. B don't like profanity, it's a sin and not lady like." Turning in Hadassah's direction she added, "and when you gon' sit down? You just gone stand there." She snarled from behind the magazine as though it provided a shield.

Hadassah had indeed been quietly standing trying to process the next step of this situation and tucking away little pockets of information.

She sat down on the bed as Nessa closed the door and a telltale click locked them in. Sam crossed her legs in lotus position and interlaced her fingers under her chin. The pose was more graceful than Hadassah imagined the girl was capable of. Sam leaned slightly over the bed to look down to the bottom of the door waiting. After several moments, footsteps retreated down the hall.

"I'm really not mean, I'm just tired of that sissy playing these fake church games."

"So where did they grab you up from?" Sam asked.

"Nichols Park. That's the last thing I remember before being here."

"Was your neck hurting?" Sam touched the side of her neck in the same place that had been aching on Hadassah for a while.

"Yeah it was", Hadassah blindly touched the spot on her neck. "How old were you?"

"Fourteen. These monsters have had me for two years. They caught me coming out of a store one morning when I was on my way to school."

"Do you have any idea where we are?" Hadassah questioned.

"I think we're still in the city, but I don't know where."

Hadassah moved to sit on the bed next Sam. "What makes you think we're still in the city?"

Sam turned to her; a downcast facial expression sent a sting of anxiety in Hadassah's heart. "You'll see. When you meet with the dates, sometimes they talk too much, especially the ones that don't want sex. They wanna talk about their wives that won't give up no booty, the jobs they hate and their bad ass kids."

Both girls chuckled.

"When they're drunk, they tell you about where they live and work. That's why I think we're still somewhere in Chicago."

"I tried to get one of them to help me one time." This time she rubbed a spot near her ribs. "Vik had Benny T beat me within two inches of my life. Then that same bastard had the nerve to request me again. He told me Vik didn't even make him pay as a thank you for telling on me. That fine church going man hurt me more than he will ever know."

Sam motioned for Hadassah to get back on her bed and laid against the pillow with her hands behind her head.

"Two years they've enslaved me, but it won't be another one." She said with a quiet confidence.

"But how can you leave?"

"I'm walking out or they gonna carry me out. But I'm not giving them another year of my mind, body, or my soul."

CHAPTER 11

For two days, Sean walked up and down the street from Washtenaw to Sacramento checking out the neighborhood. He was living in the halfway house just past the viaduct.

He threw on a navy-blue hoodie and loose-fitting jeans. As he made his way to the polish stand he spoke to a few people sitting in the courtyard. The spot didn't look too hot and he was tired of sitting on the stoop of the placement facility. There was something different about the air on that third day that made him want to move differently and get in the mix a little.

"Anybody out here selling loose squares?" he said when he came near a crowd.

"Yeah baby, I gotcha right here." A woman sitting on an orange crate with a wig that hadn't met with a comb in months, slid forward. "How many you need baby?"

He handed her two dollars. "Let me get two."

The woman let a hearty laugh and nudged the red-bone man on the crate next to her, whose head was laid against the chain link fence. "He must be new around here, still thinking cigarettes is a dollar."

The man chuckled and didn't open his eyes as he said "Homeboy, run that other dollar, smokes done went up to a buck fifty apiece"

"Dang, since when?" Sean grumbled as he fished more money from his pocket and scooped the items from her hand.

"You one of the new boys at that half-way house up the street? You just come home?"

"Yeah, something like that TeeTee," he answered using a common term on the Westside for older women still husting in the streets. "Thanks for the smokes." He moved along the path until he stood in line for a polish and fries at the Maxwell stand across the street from the Towers Housing projects, that sat in the center of the Garfield Park neighborhood.

The first week Sean was in the center, he strolled up and down the street or sat and talked with the different residents in an area they called 'The Circle' until it was time for him to check in. Most of the guys in the house had to be out looking for a job. The parole officer waived this requirement for Sean because he only had six weeks to finish out his sentence and he was then moving to another state to live with his family. The PO warned him to stay out of trouble and get through his last few weeks. Sean had gotten caught up with some guys in robbery and granted leniency when the store's camera showed him giving CPR to the clerk that was shot by one of the assailants who left him at the scene.

"What's up old-timer? Let me get two cigarettes." The morning sun was already hot. It was his first Sunday in the Center and he passed on attending the in-house church service.

He plopped down on the crate where the elderly gentleman's female companion usually sat. "Where's your girl today. I haven't seen her out here with you for a few days."

The old man sat up, resting his elbows on his knees, twisting the top off the half-pint of blue label. After a swig, "My baby's sick. That damn diabetes done start acting up again." He took a longer swig this time. "She was doing real good, but a few days ago, her sugar dropped too low and we couldn't get it back up."

The man's expression went from reflection, to question to pain. He could only wonder how long the pair had been out hustling and if they'd had a better life at another time."What's your story, son?"

The liquor under his breath was old and heavy. How could he be tipsy already? I t was only ten in the morning.

"I don't see you doing nothing but walking up and down the street. "I know you really ain't a smoker because it takes you all day to smoke two cigarettes and come back for more. You ain't a drug user either, because you walk past the drugs boys too."

Sean laughed at the man's observations because they were spot on. He made a note to keep a closer eye on this brother, now that he knew, the old man was more attuned than he had initially perceived.

"Old school, you be watching everything hunh? Why you be over here pretending to be sleep?" He took a puff on the cigarette and adjusted the crate under him. "I ain't on nothing, old man, just trying to finish out my time so I can go home."

"And where's home, because you sure don't talk like everybody else around here. You sound like you done been to school or something," The old man tipped the bottle up and drank that gin like it was bottled water. "If I didn't know any better, I think you was looking for something or somebody."

The young man's back stiffened as he took another drag from the cigarette and let the smoke billow. "Who would I be looking for? I don't know anybody around here."

The old man polished off his drink and leaned back against the fence.

"And I know you ain't looking for none them girls upstairs." He pointed up to the last building of the Towers, the building they were sitting next to.

"What girls? I haven't even seen that many girls over here." He was drunk, but he knew exactly what he was saying.

"You right, you couldn't know any of those girls, because it cost a nice little piece for an hour with one of them. That cookie cost a whole lotta cigarette money."

They both laughed, but he found nothing funny. Was he saying some girls were involved in prostitution?

As the old man spoke more about the comings and goings a shiny black escalade with government plates pulled in the small driveway between the fence and the building.

The old man closed one eye, adjusting his head in the direction of the vehicle and peered towards the man who stepped out wearing a pair of black jeans and a loose-fitting black polo shirt.

"And there's the devil himself; the Snatcher." Old School yelled, shaking the bottle in that direction.

With a big grin, the man next to the car exposed a few gold teeth.

Sean pulled the hood over his head and put his focus towards the ground before the man could get a good look at him.

CHAPTER 12

"Baby girl, how you feeling today?"

"I'm good. Ali, how come every time I come in this store it smells like spoiled meat?" The young lady at the counter clad, in pajamas, was laughing as she spoke.

"You wanna go somewhere that smells good lil' mama?" Asked the young gentleman dressed in all black and black sneakers.

"Nah, like I said I'm good. Ali, I'm tired of coming in here and it stinks."

Shayla suddenly sat up in the water, looking straight at Hadassah. "I think I'm starting to remember what happened. I was in the store and this dude was trying to talk to me. I kept brushing him off. When I walked out the store, I bumped into a guy and suddenly felt some pain in my neck. The guy in the store came out and I think he was trying to help me. It seems like I was riding in a car then I passed out. That must be how I ended up here. Damn."

Hadassah always felt eerie about the detox baths they took. The herbs Auntie Nessa used were potent and caused different memories and emotions to be released from the girls. Some of them recalled times that they had been abused, others remembered times when their lives were better. It was always a good day when the bath was just the bath.

Although Shayla had recalled her kidnapping a couple of weeks ago, today she was

complaining. "What's all this stuff in the water?" She frowned, looking into the tub with coconut milk power, hibiscus flowers and oils. Something Hadassah recognized because she was taking notes and Shayla wasn't.

"Ms. Shayla," Auntie Nessa said with an exasperated sigh. "We're never going to make it through the thirty days if there's a discussion and argument about everything, I present to you." They were now four weeks in and Auntie's frustration with Shayla was growing by the day. "I told you weeks ago I was going to be preparing different baths, oils and lotions to find the best combinations for your skin."

"I'm not arguing," Shayla protested in a huff, "I'm just asking a question." She finally got undressed and stepped into the water, but pulled back "Damn, why is this water so hot?"

Hadassah used her fingers to check the water and found it to be a scalding temperature. But she had to endure it anyway; their special baths didn't end until the water was cold. The rest of the experience took place in tense quiet.

Auntie Nessa was helping the girls dry off in another special room when she spoke. "Ms. Brittany, we're coming up on one month and you haven't had a period. You haven't had no dates yet, and you were still a virgin when we checked you, so I'm trying to see what's going on."

Brittany's eyes watered instantly. She looked back and forth between Hadassah and Auntie. She slumped against the wall with the spa towel still wrapped around her body. "He said I had to," she cried and her voice trembled. Hadassah gripped her own towel tightening it because she knew bad news would follow.

"He told me Benny T would beat me if I didn't do it." Auntie Nessa stepped in front of Brittany, moving past Shayla, adjusting the girls' towel as though trying to keep her anger at bay. "Who, is he? Baby what are you talking about?" "Van," Brittany screamed. "Van's been having sex with me every day since we been here. He comes to get me at night when you go to your room."

She was now leaning against the wall as though she could disappear. "He takes me in the stairwell and bends me over like I'm a dog or something." Her shoulders heaved with the weight of that confession. "He kept telling me I couldn't tell nobody, not even you. He said he would kill me and you too."

Auntie Nessa swallowed hard, the grip on the towel lightened, but only a little.

"And it looks like this sneaky little bastard done got you pregnant." Auntie shook her head and mumbled, "Betrayal; always from within."

She reached for Brittany who looked ready to pass out.

Hadassah released a breath, afraid for Brittany. They took so much pride because she was a virgin. What would happen to her friend now?

"Come here baby." When Auntie hugged Brittany, the girl released a moan that made Hadassah's skin crawl. She moved Brittany away and directed her to put on the clothes that were laid out on the chair.

"Auntie's gonna take care of everything." She lit a cigarette and took two long pulls. "It's gonna be hell for Van to pay as good as Vik's been to him. And he knows virgins command a high price. He could have taken another beauty instead, but he took the one Vik was basing his next cash haul on. So rare to get virgins these days."

She put her focus on Hadassah. "Dark and Lovely you and Shayla gon' ahead to your rooms. I'll come and get you later for help with dinner. Come on baby, finish putting on these clothes."

She helped Brittany finish dressing and escorted her to her room as they went in the opposite direction.

Hadassah didn't know if she should talk about what happened or not, she came in and stretched out on her bed, keeping her expression neutral.

Sam was sitting with her back against the wall when Hadassah came in. Van had also come to her with promises to help her escape, but she called his bluff. That man wouldn't kill anyone. Too much money was riding on them. He tried to get physically rough with her, but the moment she said Auntie Nessa will want to know where the bruises came from, he backed off.

Sam's sly grin was infuriating. "So you ain't gotta say nothing," she taunted "I knew somebody was gone find out that Van been screwing that girl since y'all got here. The question is what's about to happen. Vik B is from the deep south and he don't believe in abortion." She released a cackle that made Hadassah flinch. "Ain't that a crock, because you shole don't see no babies around here, do you?" He was late with this crew. Van usually hits before the examination. That's why virgins have been hard for them to find. He's been popping cherries, forcing them to get more girls to meet the demand.

Hadassah sat up so fast her head was spinning. "So, you knew Van was having sex with her?"

"Chile, everybody knew," Sam replied with a dismissive wave. "It was only a matter of time before he popped her off. He was raw dogging her every chance he got, what else was gonna happen?" She laughed as she snatched up another magazine and put her head on her pillow.

Hadassah laid back again, wiping a tear trailing from the corner of her eye. *Had he also done the same to Shayla?* "What's gonna happen to Brittany and her baby?"

Sam slid off the bed and moved across the room to kneel next to Hadassah. She glanced over to the bottom of the door to make sure no one was listening in.

"When one of them gets pregnant, they take them in a van and drop them off in another state and just leave them. They make sure they can't trace anything back here." She checked the bottom of the door again. "Benny T had been trying to get Vik to sell the babies on the Black Market, but Vik wanted no parts of it." She slid back to her bed and continued reading as if she hadn't said a word.

That was the last day Hadassah saw Brittany or Van. She didn't dare ask anything else. One day she would find out because everyone in the Bayou loved to talk. Gossip among the girls at dinner time was how she learned more about the happenings in this place.

The thirty days of detoxing and skin treatments was almost over, and she had not given up, but now she had to focus on preparing to lose her virginity and virtue to men that would pay to have sex with her. Thoughts of school and family had been pushed to the background; too painful to entertain. The one thing she held onto was the prayers her grandmother had taught her to pray. She would never stop asking God to please deliver her out of this trouble.

CHAPTER 13

Screams pierced the air and Sean picked up speed. When he made it to the circle, the woman referred to as TeeTee was flailing her arms, screaming and pointing to the man with the gold teeth. He was leaning against the familiar shiny Escalade, watching.

"What's going on?" Sean asked a random guy standing in the crowd.

"Bro, somebody slit Old School's throat and left him laying against the fence. TeeTee walked up this morning and found him. I think he had been out here all night. She been screaming at The Snatcher and he's just been laughing at her."

Sirens blared in the distance. Old School was propped up against the fence, as he was every day. Every ounce of blood in his body covered the thin jacket draped across his small frame. Minutes later TeeTee was still screaming and pointing towards The Snatcher, who looked as though he didn't have a care in the world. The paramedics arrived with a stretcher and moved people out of the way to get to the victim.

TeeTee hurled profanities at the gold-toothed man, who was now becoming frustrated with her accusations, as he was walked towards her with a frown that matched his vibe. Sean's interest had been peeked about the girls Old School had mentioned and wondered what was really going on in the Towers.

"Look, look now he's coming for me," she screeched, wagging a bony finger at the man. "What you gon' do Snatcher? Cut my throat too? Right out here in front of everybody? Or are you gonna wait till night time like you did my man?"

The paramedics paused in calling for a medical examiner and put their focus on The Snatcher. Sean stepped in front of the Snatcher and glanced over his shoulder to a woman standing close by.

"Get TeeTee and walk away so she can talk to the paramedics."

The Snatcher glared at Sean with eyes empty and cold as he growled, "Man, you don't know me, so you betta get out of my way and get out my business."

"Aye man, it's already heat out here." Sean shot back, still blocking the path to TeeTee. "We ain't tryna be under police surveillance all day, every day. You know if you hit her, the paramedics have to call the police. I'll take care of her, just gon' in the building so everybody out here can go back to getting their money."

The man's gaze swept across the onlookers who were focused on him. His face softened when he took in the paramedics requesting a police presence. "Yeah, alright young blood, y'all betta get her." He was standing toe to toe and almost nose to nose with Sean before conceding. When he turned and walked back to the Escalade, Sean released a long steady breath.

People inched away from the action, going back to what they were doing before this ugly scene occurred. Sean helped TeeTee pick up all Old school's belongings and took them to the tiny apartment they shared just down the street on Washtenaw.

She was still distraught, but wasn't crying as much. He looked around the well-kept apartment. A tan couch cover and floral pillow decorated the oversize couch with thick wooden legs. There was a military picture of a man hanging over the small dining room table covered with a thick plastic tablecloth; a wooden chair on each side. The eyes of the man in the photograph were no doubt Old School's. Noticing Sean looking at the picture TeeTee spoke, "Yeah, Old School did two tours in Vietnam. He was never quite right after that, but he never lost that sharp mind." She chuckled as she put his things away. "A lot of people that are always in the circle always knew there was something different about him, always asking him what they should do." She smiled as she thought of her man.

"TeeTee, I'm going to need you to be safe, that man is straight up evil." Sean said stuffing his hands in his pockets.

"Thank you, Sean. I'ma stay outta the circle for a minute. You know, get Old School buried and everything." She then mumbled something about having insurance. "I think I might go live with my sister, for a while." She placed a reassuring hand on this shoulder. "The Snatcher looked like he actually was going to hurt me, thank you for stepping in." He placed his hand over hers.

"No problem, TeeTee. Going away sounds like a good idea. You don't want that dude to catch you by yourself."

Sean finished stacking everything in the corner TeeTee had directed him to.

"You take care, I'ma get back over to The Circle and see what else is going on."

"Hold on a minute."

TeeTee went to a back room and returned with three cartons of cigarettes. "You can have these and hold down the corner 'till I get back." Sean took the boxes and tapped them against each other. "My name's Marlene. I know everybody use TeeTee, but that's the name my mama gave me." His eyes landed on some awards on the opposite wall. She was smiling and Sean realized at that moment he hadn't seen her teeth. Somewhere in her early life she was a real good-looking lady with a big heart. Though her eyes held a sadness he understood.

"You sure TeeTee, I know you done built that corner up. It's your empire. Pretty big shoes to fill."

They both laughed.

"I'm sure baby and you be careful too. You know the Snatcher hurt my man because he knew what he was doing. One thing that always bothered Old School was that he couldn't help them girls. Police wouldn't listen. No one did anything. He always saw him bringing in them girls. Some of them girls been up there for years."

"Years? For real?" Sean questioned.

She nodded, as her words trailed off.

"Some of them don't make it out alive."

CHAPTER 14

*H*adassah, unlike Shayla and Brittany had somehow won favor with Auntie Nessa and was assigned to be her apprentice. Could be because she understood how to play along until she could find a way out. Nothing good would come out of making these people upset.

"Baby, I've been taking care of this place for ten years now. Auntie's getting tired." She clasped her large hands together. "I know this ain't a easy situation to be in, but I've been watching you take it all in stride. You ain't a crybaby like the rest of 'em either; that's something special."

"Does that mean I won't have to have any dates?" Hadassah had been hearing some dreadful stories from some girls about the things their dates wanted them to do. All of this was a far cry from going to college, starting a career, finding a husband, having children and living a happy life. Some girls had been with so many men they had lost count. Some had come from decent homes like Hadassah's while others had troubled lives and this was an actual step up from their situations.

"We'll see. Vik wants to put someone in Cecelia's place. Part of that job is sleeping with Vik and Vik only - on demand."

Hadassah was separating the herbs to use in their baths. She glanced up at Auntie, then back down to the task at hand. "Is it gonna hurt?" Auntie paused for several moments. "Well baby girl let's put it like this." She placed a hand on Hadassah to halt her movement.

"It might hurt to you because you aint' never had nothing up in you. But from what I hear, that li'l chicken nugget he got, you'll be okay when you leave this place." She winked and started laughing so loud that Hadassah laughed too, though it did not seem funny on any level. By paying close attention to Auntie Nessa, she had also learned the answer to Shayla's question. No matter how made up, regally dressed; certain physical things gave it away.

She had finished sorting and was putting the herbs in small tea bags. She stopped, thought about what Auntie said and looked her square in the face.

"Sam said she's been here for two years, Cecelia five and you ten. Is this how my life is gonna end?" The thought of being Auntie's helper was now overshadowed by never leaving the Bayou.

"You have to learn how to play the cards life deals you, not the ones you hope are in the deck." Auntie Nessa lit a cigarette and relaxed against the chair. "All I can tell you is, there's a scripture that says all things must end. You'd be surprised how things suddenly come to pass around here." Now Hadassah was leaning forward. "But why are you still here."

After a long long pull on the cigarette, Auntie released the smoke with a sigh. "You don't get to do whatever you want with your life." She leaned toward Hadassah, put the cigarette in her direction. "You only get so much anyway," Auntie Nessa said, "especially as a Black woman."

If she had timed things correctly, Hadassah had been imprisoned in the Bayou for forty-five days. She still had not met with Vik after her thirty days of beauty treatments and detox and she had not been on any dates. She spent her days preparing food, making baths, working in the greenhouse and learning how to make lotions and blend oils. Her thoughts often drifted to her parents and what life would have been like had they not died. They had met at the University of Pennsylvania. It always made her smile to think of how special her father must have been for her mother to go against her parents and her Muslim background to marry her father and move to Chicago. Hadassah wondered how her grandmother was holding up. She had suffered so much loss; losing her husband, her son and daughter-in-law and now her only grandchild was missing. Hadassah was sure Mama Betty was angrier with God than ever. She still believed that because of her prayers she would somehow make it back to her family.

Hadassah had learned so much about Auntie Nessa, who was born in a deep, rural area in Mississippi as Ernest Ferguson. Life was good in the south living with his grandma Myrtis. As a young boy, he learned all about beauty treatments, notions, potions and concoctions. Women in their town and surrounding areas would come to Myrtis to get help with any desire they had for a man.

His grandmother had accepted the decision for him to live as a 'she' but warned him that not everyone would. Growing up in the south as a Black gay man, was a fight on the same level as dealing with the Klan. All was fair in love and potions until grandma fell asleep one night with the stove still going. The house and everything in it were burned to a crisp. They found Ernest in the crawl space huddled with his grandmother's potions and recipe books.

Grandma's baby sister, Aunt Elnora came with her husband to get him two days later, taking him to Chicago right after the memorial service, leaving Mississippi behind for good.

Auntie Nessa took on a new name and identified as a woman once in Chicago. His holy roller, bible thumping Auntie Elnora and her husband had a hard time accepting his becoming a 'her'. She tried to beat the 'she' out of him and eventually put him out. Nessa found work as an extra in a drag show to make money. Her room, down the hallway from the kitchen, was full of beautiful flashy clothes, tons of jewelry and so many wigs, Hadassah couldn't count them. Nessa landed in a subsidized unit in the Towers and had been there for over twenty years.

"One day Viktor sent a message through one his errand boys

asking me to come to his office. When I got there, he said he heard I was taking in girls and letting them stay with me and that was against the housing program's rules."

She sat back with the lit cigarette. "I told him straight to his face. These girls is out here tricking and everything else. They ain't got nowhere to go. I help them and fix them up when they done had a bad time."

She leaned forward on her elbows and sighed. "He made a deal with me right then and there. He said I can live rent free and earn some money if I helped him with the business, he was starting with the girls he was bringing in."

She shrugged "I thought about it for a few days and was like what the hell? Free rent, taking care of girls is what I was doing anyway. Why not? She took a long drag off the cigarette and watched the smoke billow into the air. The stories Auntie told always enthralled Hadassah and on a strange note she was glad Nessa had found a place in the world to be who she wanted to be and do what she loved.

"I had no idea I'd be here ten years later, seeing all that I've seen." She chuckled, but there was no warmth in it.

"Yeah baby, Auntie Nessa's still here. She dumped the ashes in the crystal ashtray that was always on the table. "Enough story time. Let's get done so we can get this dinner started. I'm making veggie lasagna tonight."

While Auntie had settled in to be under Vik's thumb, Hadassah never would. Even with special treatment and favor, Hadassah still longed for home. She wanted to see her uncles, grandmother and all her cousins. How long would it be before she could go back to her family?

Now at almost forty-five days of being a prisoner, her hope was already waning. Would they still love her after the things she would be forced to do? If gossip held true, there were still things happening in the Bayou that no one spoke upon. Things like Brittany exposing that Van had been sleeping with her and she had gotten pregnant; Brittany nor Van were seen or mentioned again.

CHAPTER 15

$\mathcal{A}$nticipation and energy were high. All dates had been cancelled for the long-awaited trip outside the Bayou. Even though Hadassah had been there nearly two months, the unfortunate situation with Van and Brittany and some old guy being killed outside the building had prevented the two previously scheduled outings.

Benny T lined all the girls up in the hallway and gave them a hard look. "We're going out in the field today. Don't try to escape because when I catch you it is going to cost you." He smiled as though nothing would please him more. "Just enjoy the day, and have a good time on your day off."

"For the newbies, the windows on the van are blacked out on purpose," Auntie Nessa chimed in, moving her hands in Benny T's direction. "There are no signs or any clues of where we'll be. We've had girls try and leave clues for someone to find us in the past. Let me just say, those girls are no longer with us."

Shayla and Hadassah shared a nervous glance. "Anybody have questions?" Not a single hand went up. Everyone understood questions were discouraged. Hadassah counted nine floor landings as they marched down the stairs. They seemed to be in a project building like the one some of her cousins lived in. The walls along the staircase were all cinderblock and faint signs of life from the residents echoed around them. A warm breeze on her legs and face was exhilarating as they stepped over the threshold of the red brick building directly into a custom oversized minibus. A small bus had been designed to fit three girls to a seat.

This was Hadassah's first time outside since the day she was abducted and she was overwhelmed with emotion between the spaces of enjoying the outing and the sadness of missing home. This was the one time a month they would be outside.

The air-conditioned drive was comfortable. Three chattering girls to each cushioned seat reminded Hadassah of field trips on the big yellow school buses, taking her to place like Museum of Science and Industry, the Adler Planetarium, and the Shedd Aquarium. There was so much talking and laughing going on, before she knew it, they were backing into a spot and Benny T was telling everyone to get ready to unload.

Nessa and Benny T gave each girl a blanket, a lunch box, bottles of water and iced tea. They spread the blankets on freshly cut grass and took up whatever positions made them comfortable. Some stretched out and soaked up the sun, others sat on wooden benches to chat with each other. This was the first time Hadassah had seen all of the girls in a natural element. They had on no make-up, no lashes, no lipstick or rouge. The care that Auntie Nessa had given them was unmistakable. Even in the natural, every girl was beautiful. If she hadn't known were she was, she could have sworn they were on a college campus between classes.

Shayla, scooted to the edge of her blanket where it touched Hadassah's. "Do you have any idea where we are?"

Hadassah shook her head, but said nothing since Benny T was watching them more closely than the others.

"There's lots of woods. I'm thinking if I ran and hid deep enough in the trees, they would only look for me for so long. We were only riding for about forty-five minutes, so we can't be that far from any part of the city."

Hadassah's head whipped in her direction. "Girl are you crazy? Did you forget that we haven't seen Brittany or Van again? Not a peep."

Sam was suddenly standing barefoot on the blanket with Shayla, looking between both of them and back at Benny T. He was smoking on a cigar and drinking from a silver flask. He seemed quite comfortable in his oversized fold-up chair, listening to the sounds of the music coming from the open doors of the bus, but his focus was still on the newbies.

"I already know what you're over here talking about Shayla. And I advise you to get it out your head." She turned a warning glare on Hadassah. "And don't you be no fool and let this fool make a fool out of you."

Shayla glanced in Benny T's direction before she spoke, "Girl, ain't nobody trying to just be stuck here forever."

Sam stooped down and reached out to put her hand on Shayla's shoulder. "More than anyone, I want to get out of this place. But I'm also not trying to die to get my freedom. Every girl that has tried to escape, it turned out bad. I'm just telling you, don't try it."

Shayla snatched away, came to her feet, and tightened her ponytail held together by a white stretchy band and started to walk away from both girls.

Sam stood as well. "Don't do it Sis, please." Sam whispered as loud as she could without drawing any attention as Shayla stalked from the blanket.

When it was time to leave, Benny T yelled, "Make sure you have all your stuff. Fold up your blankets and stack them in that spot." He pointed to a place where the doors were open. Auntie Nessa held open a big black garbage bag for each girl to dispose of their trash before they stepped in to take the same seats there were in before.

Everyone was situated when Auntie Nessa started calling out each name. She called Shayla's name twice and no answer. The seat where she sat on the drive in was empty.

Fear gripped Hadassah's heart at the thought of Shayla running and hiding in the woods. She didn't even remember the moment she crept off.

Sam locked gazes with Hadassah and there was no mistaking the tear that escaped down the other girl's face.

CHAPTER 16

"Hey young blood, let me holla at you for a minute." The Snatcher had been keeping a low profile since the public accusations of Old School's murder. Sean had been holding down the cigarette spot just like he promised TeeTee. He was also making sure to lay low in case his parole officer drove through Harrison Street. The regulars in the circle expressed missing Old School and TeeTee and the wisdom they provided that only the people that frequented the circle knew about. Sean walked over to the gold toothed gentleman in the small driveway.

"Yeah, wassup man? What you need?" The man gave him a once over.

"You looking for a job? We need to replace one of our security people."

"Yeah, I'm interested," Sean leaned in. "What do I have to do and what's the pay?"

"Hold on brother, slow down," the Snatcher said with a chuckle. "I'ma come down here tonight about eight once it gets dark. I'ma take you up to have an interview with the big boss."

"Bet, I'll be right here," Sean said glancing up at the building, realizing his life was about to change.

Later that evening. Benny T stepped from the steel door and motioned for Sean to come inside the building. The reconstruction of the stair case and elevator intrigued Sean. "Man, how did y'all pull this off? You guys have completely cut off the first eight floors. You can't even tell there's a whole other side."

"Yeah, it is hooked up ain't it? Boss man used that fancy engineering degree he has to hide us away from everybody else." Benny T, spoke slowly, leaning, while he waited for the elevator to get to the ninth floor.

Sean's potential new boss was a tall, impeccably dressed gentleman with a deep accent. The wall behind his desk was decorated with frame after frame of awards and photos with celebrities and politicians. He reached across the desk, to shake Sean's hand and then reclaimed his spot in the executive chair while motioning for Sean and Benny T to have a seat.

"So my head security here tells me you prevented a situation the other day that could have gone incredibly bad." He cupped his chin, placing the knuckle of his index finger under his bottom lip. "I thank you for stepping in helping to calm down that temper of his." Sean glanced over at The Snatcher who was grinning like he'd won the lottery.

"You're welcome." Sean nodded and locked in on his host. "It was no problem."

Viktor reached for a clip board on his desk.

"So let's get right to it. It seems like you're living in the Second Time Around rehabilitation center just east of here on Harrison Street, that correct?"

"Yeah, I just came home from Vandalia." Sean replied, wondering how much information they had on him since he'd only been given the offer a few hours ago. They must have checked beforehand.

Vik moved his chair back, interlacing his fingers on the top knee of his crossed legs. "Okay, so what are your plans after that?"

"I haven't thought about all that yet." Sean kept his focus on Vik as he realized that looking away would be viewed as a sign of weakness.

"I just been out here doing a little hustling nothing too dramatic that might draw attention." Vik looked at the Snatcher who shrugged.

"Let me present this to you for your consideration," Vik said. "You can come work for us every day starting at twelve noon until 8:30pm. That gives you seven hours, plus breaks and enough time to get back to the center. The pay is five hundred a week cash, for now."

Sean slid to the edge of the seat. "You for real? Five hundred a week? To do what?"

Vik stood and smoothed the front of his houndstooth tailor-made suit.

"If you agree to our terms, come here tomorrow at twelve. I'll have another one of our employees help you complete all necessary forms and documents. Please bring your ID and we will walk you through your daily duties. Any questions?" Vik stood and buttoned the front of his jacket. He wouldn't receive an answer to the question he wanted.

Benny T stood and Sean followed suit, realizing the meeting was over. "Thank you, Mister, what do you want me to call you?"

Vik extended his hand. "My name is Viktor Batista, President of the Towers. See you tomorrow." He moved away to reclaim the seat behind the desk and opened his laptop. He didn't look up as they left the office.

Once down stairs, Benny T held out this fist and Sean touched his own to Benny's. "See you tomorrow man, good looking out.",

"Same here. I hope you got a strong stomach, Benny T said as a warning; the only one he would get. "This work you about to get into ain't for the weak."

Sean closed down the cigarette corner for the night so he could get rested and be ready for the next day. He didn't know what tasks he would be assigned, but working in the Towers would beat working the cigarette corner on any day.

CHAPTER 17

They had summoned all nineteen girls to the kitchen early the next morning after the outing.

"So you know it's gon' be hell for all of us to pay for Shayla, right, I told you not to let her do it." Sam was pulling on a pair of leggings and t-shirt. Hadassah followed suit, throwing on something and glossing her lips.

"You think cause you Vik's number one pick right now and Auntie's helper you're safe?" Sam asked with a snicker. "We're all in the same boat when the pot gets stirred."

Sam was pulling on socks and comfortable shoes. "Do you think you're leaving here? They make cash money off us being on our backs. Why would they let us go? Better get used to it."

Sam hit the bars by the single window that still existed. Hadassah could hear the panic growing as her voice rose. "We can't even see out of the window, let alone raise it up and call for help. You betta let go of this *leaving here* fantasy real quick."

"But what if we all sa-."

"Say what? What do you want to say?" Sam was now bending in front of Hadassah with a grip on her upper arms that sent pain shooting up to Hadassah's shoulders. "Say what. Vik, Shayla was ready to leave and I've been here long enough, it's time for me to go too?" Tears were streaming down her face, and she was almost screaming. "Don't you get it. You've been around here playing like you're at summer camp or something. Girl, we are trapped. We are being sold for thousands of dollars, and we won't see a dime. The only way out is death. Wake up girl, wake u-."

The door to their room opened. Benny T was standing in the doorway with his usual infuriating grin. Both girls froze. "What's the hold up?"

Sam wiped her face with a shaky hand, smoothed her hair back into place and tried to move past him. "Everything is fine, we gotta meet in the kitchen." He blocked her path. "Can I get pass? I need to go to the bathroom first."

"Sure, go right ahead." He stepped to the side. "And make it quick, both of you. Remember this ain't no damn summer camp." Fear set in as she pretended to straighten up the already made bed. Benny T's words served as a reminder that someone was always listening. "I'm coming right now." Her words stammering from her lips.

"Vik wants you to sit right next to him at the table," he said in a deceptive tone that struck fear in Hadassah's mind. *Why? Why would that man want me there?*

Vik was already sitting at the head of the table when the last few girls scampered to get in. He smiled then signaled for Hadassah to take the space to his right. She complied, kept her gaze down and moved into the chair without making a sound.

Vik stood up and scanned the expectant faces. He cleared his throat and touched a hand to his chest. "It truly pains me to see that someone didn't feel good about staying in the Bayou. It appears by her sudden disappearance that she no longer wanted to be a part of our wonderful family." He reached down and gently stroked Hadassah' hair.

"It also seems that someone may have known that she was going to leave." He snatched Hadassah's head back and pain shot up her neck. Then twisted a full lock of hair turning her face to his; looking her square in the eye, but she could barely see through her tears. His voice was slow, words articulate and without any concealed anger. "Did you know what she was planning to do?"

She tried shaking her head but his grip was too tight. In one motion Benny T was standing next to Sam and gripped a lock of her hair in the same manner. "I saw her talking to you, did she tell you she was leaving?" Sam grabbed his hand with both her hands and tried to move the chair. Benny T gripped harder, then pushed her and the chair into the table before slamming her head down so her cheek smashed against the table. The more she moved, the harder he pressed until she stopped moving.

"I saw her talking to you and this other trick," he pointed in Hadassah's direction. "I'm going to ask you again, did you know?"

"No," Sam screamed through tears, "No!"

Vik said "That's enough."

He then unraveled his hand from Hadassah's hair and stepped back. Benny T copied his motion. Sam remained in place for a minute crying while Vik began speaking.

"I guess we're not going to get any answers from anyone today. So, we have a response for you." Slightly nodding to his head of security.

Benny T pulled a small black plastic bag from his pocket and tossed the contents on the middle of the table.

Gasps and shrieks echoed around the room. Some girls looked away, others grabbed their mouths or stomachs, some backed away as far as possible. Hadassah peered at the ponytail, still being held together by a white holder, and a patch of scalp, covered in blood.

Vik sat down, smoothing his designer tie and jacket. "It will do you all well to understand there is no escaping." His voice sounded so menacing, some girls could not contain their tears or sobs.

"Oh come come now," he taunted "Let's dry up these unnecessary tears."

Silence instantly fell over the room.

"I'm not going to have a long discussion about this incident," Vik said, gesturing for everyone to simmer down. "First Van, then Brittany, now Shayla. So much betrayal in so little time. I have a new member of our security team starting later today."

He cleared his throat again. "But I am going to say this. Let's not have a repeat of what they did. Every ass in here is for sale. There are no side deals or arrangements. If someone comes to you with something that isn't quite right, please advise Auntie Nessa or Benny T." He let those words settle in, but the fear remained.

"Is everyone clear on everything I just said."

Everyone nodded, some mumbled their consent.

He stood and flicked his wrist looking at an expensive watch.

Everyone stood to leave, including Hadassah. Unfortunately, he grabbed her arm, pulling her close to him. "You're going with me today."

He smiled, stood and pushed in her chair, signaling for her to walk in front of him.

Hadassah glanced at Auntie Nessa who nodded with a smile that didn't reach her eyes.

CHAPTER 18

*H*adassah was perched on the side of her bed, rubbing her hands up and down her thighs. She did not know what to expect, how to dress or fix her hair. Vik had only said, "You're coming with me." What did that mean? Where were they going? How long would they be there? Was tonight the night she had been dreading? She chose a simple turquoise jersey dress from her dresser.

Sam's eyes were still swollen from crying in the kitchen. "What's wrong with you? Why are you sitting there in a daze?" She propped herself up on her elbow.

Hadassah looked at Sam without seeing her. "Vik told me I'm going with him today. I don't know what's going to happen."

Sam moved over next to her on the bed wrapping her arms around her shoulders. "Today is most likely the day he's going to take your virginity. The best thing I can tell you is to think of something that makes you happy. Focus on that the entire time. It's going to hurt a little bit but not for long. I've heard from one of the other girls he slept with that he does his business quick and falls asleep."

Hadassah couldn't see Sam with tears pooling in her eyes. "Sam, I'm scared."

Sam leaned in with a hug. "I know you are. I hope for your sake it'll be over quick."

The door opened and Auntie Nessa was standing there. "Come on Dark and Lovely, Vik is ready to go."

Hadassah gave Sam a big hug before she stood and wiped her face. Sam whispered "think happy thoughts" as she left the room closing the door behind her.

Though the windows were dark, Hadassah could tell they had gotten on the expressway by the speed Benny T was driving. When she stepped from the truck, they entered a side door.

The house was spotless with a southern feel to it. Soft music was playing in the background. He directed her to a bathroom, "Wash your hands and then come down the hallway when you're done." She followed his direction and made her way to the dining room where the table had been set for two. A single white candle was lit in the center and food on the table ready to be served. This looked more like a romantic dinner for a dating couple. She inhaled and released a deep breath as her thoughts came back to what this was; her first time would be with a man who had taken her from her family, locked her away from the world and his only concern was she would bring him money.

Vik walked to her and motioned her to sit in the chair he held out for her. He gently spread the cloth napkin on her lap and poured them both a glass of wine from the bottle in the silver ice bucket. No regard for the fact that she was years below the legal drinking age. Evidently rules did not apply here.

"So you had planned all this since this morning?" she questioned.

"My housekeeper Maria set everything up as we arrived; we couldn't have any unattended candles burning now, could we?" He smiled a charming one that didn't seem as sinister as other times.

He served them both the delicious smelling food. "Make sure you don't tell Auntie Nessa that we had steak." He laughed as he cut into the thick T-bone.

"You haven't tried your wine yet. Take a sip, it has a sweetness to it

I think you'll like," he said diving into the loaded baked potato. "I-, I don't drink wine," she stammered.

"I know you don't just try it. I'm pretty sure you'll like it after a few sips. Let it sit on your palate."

Hadassah understood that Vik's suggestions were more like commands. She picked up the glass and took a small sip then set the glass back down.

"How was that?" he asked, taking a sip of his own dark red wine.

"Not bad, a little sweet."

"All right then." He lightly tapped his fork and knife together, still smiling.

"Drink up. We don't want this delicious wine to go to waste."

The conversation was light, and soon Hadassah felt the effects of the wine, which was more than she thought it would be, given the fact it taste like a sparkling juice.

When they both finished their meal and the entire bottle of wine, Vik helped her stand. "Let me give you a tour of the house." She felt a heavy wave of dizziness when she got to her feet. He held her while pushing in the chair.

"Let's start with the parlor."

She could hear him speaking and could see what was in front of her, but couldn't feel her feet against the floor as she walked.

When they reached the bedroom. He led her to an oversized chair in one corner.

"I'm going to freshen up a bit."

He stepped into a bathroom and she thought it was strange to hear him humming as the water ran. After about ten minutes, he came out in a white tank top and black silk pajama pants.

She froze, trying to decide which emotion to feel while he gently brought her to her feet and pulled her close to him. The wine had her relaxed and unafraid, but a small part of her brain reminded her of what was about to happen and that she had every reason to be fearful. This was not what she wanted.

He rubbed her shoulders and whispered, "Hadassah, I know you're afraid, but you don't have to be."

She looked into his eyes and even through the cloudiness, she saw softness in his eyes for the first time. It still did not seem right.

"I don't want t-,"

"Here, let me help you take off your dress."

CHAPTER 19

Three days had passed since Hadassah's horrific night with Viktor. As much as Vik attempted to make it a romantic evening, the truth was still the truth. Auntie Nessa had not prepared her for the wave of emotions that came afterwards; guilt, fear, hurt and loneliness. If this is what her life had become, death seemed to be a better option.

Since then, they had given her an extra hour to sleep in the mornings and it was official she was being groomed to be "Queen Beauty" to replace Cecelia. She spent most of that extra hour praying and thinking of her family. Hadassah knew her grandmother was in a fit and hoped her uncles Derek and Louis were keeping Mama Betty from running her blood pressure up with worry. With this new title came new privileges. She would be allowed to go outside to the store with Auntie Nessa or the new security guard who she had yet to meet. Auntie Nessa informed her she would meet the new guy sometime today.

"I sure hope you don't think you're something special now. It's only a matter of time before Vik turns on you too." Sam smirked as she wrapped her hair in Bantu knots, sitting cross-legged on her bed. "He is a narcissistic, HBCU educated, pimp from the New Orleans

Bayou, dressed up as a politician running a ho' house right up under everybody's nose."

"Why do you always have to be so bitter?" Hadassah asked, realizing there was a bit of jealousy in Sam's voice. "We are in a messed-up situation as it is and we're all trying to make the best of it."

"Is that what we're calling it now? Sam said with a laugh. "Making the best of it. Girl please. You done got brainwashed like some of these other ones. Thinking because they here, it's better than being in foster home after foster home or out on the street. I've had enough of this "making the best of it and when Benny T take-."

Hadassah turned her full body in Sam's direction to find out why she had stopped cold in the middle of her sentence. "When Benny T takes what?"

Sam peered down to see if anyone was standing at the door. Then motioned for Hadassah to come sit on her bed; which she did. "Benny T has been planning to take Vik out for a while now. He's working with some people that want to get their hands on this Bayou gold mine." She leaned over and checked the door again. "How do you think I know so much about what's going on? Benny T is my man girl, you haven't figured that out by now?" Hadassah shook her head, realizing she'd been slipping. How did she miss this too?

"So, while you're all smiles and bedmates with Mr. Vik, keep your eyes and ears open." She shooed Hadassah off her bed, "Now gon', I been talking too much," then picked up the comb and resumed knotting her hair.

Hadassah moved back to her bed tucking that information away as she and laid down for a quick nap before sliding into the kitchen to help Auntie Nessa prepare lunch. Before drifting off to sleep, she pondered if she would ever tell Sam that Benny T had come on to her as well with promises of him becoming the big boss and her being his leading lady. She called the same bluff on him as she had on Van, to expose him to Auntie Nessa.

a hard knock on the door awakened Hadassah from her nap. "Vik wants you to come to his office, right away," said the voice on the other side. She didn't pretend to think he meant it for her roommate.

Sam smirked as she turned on her side. "Gon' get up now, Queen Bee, you've been summoned."

Hadassah slid on her shoes and opened the door to find Benny T standing with his usual wicked grin and hands in his pockets. Unlike Sam, she had the freedom to move about, so she didn't understand what he was waiting for.

"Gon' head, I'm right behind you," he said. "I need to get Sam ready to go upstairs for her next date." She felt a tug in her stomach with his words but ignored it and made her way to Vik's office.

The moment she stepped across the threshold he looked up. "Come in darling. I want you to meet the new security guy that's going to be helping Benny T since we had to let Van go."

The new guy was dressed in a long sleeve fitted blue t-shirt and baggy blue jeans. The muscular shape of his arms looked as if he worked out on the regular. His low-cut dark hair was wavy and shiny, complimenting his dark chocolate complexion.

"Hadassah meet Sean. Sean, please stand and greet our new Queen Bee, Hadassah." Sean moved from the chair and faced her. She bit her lip and tasted blood.

"Hi," was all she could manage. He gave her a stoic gaze. "Hey how are you doing?" He put both hands in his pockets then shifted his focus to Vik.

Hadassah had to control her facial expression as she tried to contain her shock. She stopped the smile, but the tears almost gave her away. Vik walked over to her, his gaze flickering between her and Sean. She rubbed her eyes with both hands.

"I'm okay, it seems like something is bothering my eyes, some fresh oil or something."

"Come on and sit down," Vik softly touching her elbow to guide her to the oversized soft leather seat. During their first night together, Vik had expressed how much he had been watching her since she arrived. He told her he had preferred her more than the others, because she accepted her situation with a grace and humility, he found endearing. The ones who held out hope were always tiresome. He said she gave him the opportunity to be his true self. If only he could see inside her mind, he would know how well her uncle had prepared her.

When she took a seat in the chair next to Sean she kept her head down. Everything Vik said sounded like the voice from a Charlie Brown movie. Her mind was filled with one thought; 'My uncle Derek has found me.' She couldn't believe that he was sitting right here next to her.

But why was Vik calling him Sean?

"Hadassah, hello." Vik snapped, his frustration evident in his voice and expression. She lifted her head to Vik glaring at her.

"Are you listening to me?"

"Yes, I'm sorry, I don't know what's wrong with my eyes," measuring her words and using the bottom of her shirt to wipe away those frustrating tears.

Vik lifted the phone from the cradle. "Auntie, can you bring something for Hadassah's eyes? They're burning for some reason." Vik put an intense gaze on Hadassah before disconnecting the call. "She's on her way. "I'll be right back."

"Okay," she said, still trying to get her emotions under control.

As soon as the door closed, she couldn't help but throw her arms around her uncle's neck. He yanked her arms down, glanced at the door before looking her directly in the face. "There could be cameras in here."

She whispered, "No, there isn't any in this room because he doesn't want anything that happens in here to incriminate him."

"I'm undercover. We don't have that much time to get you and these girls out of here. Benny T has a plan to move Vik out so he can move up. I don't know how this is going to play out. You have to be very careful and pick up on anything and everything I say. Do you understand?"

"But how did you find me?" she was still whispering, "What's about to ha-." Auntie Nessa burst in with a small container of coconut oil. "Here. What's going on with your eyes?"

"I don't know," she said taking the oil and coated both her eyes.

"Hey boy, you're a real handsome fella." Auntie Nessa squeezed Sean's shoulder. Don't be in here looking at the New Queen Bee, it'll cost you your head."

Sean frowned as he gave Auntie Nessa a once over. "You don't have to worry about that, I have a grown woman. This little girl is too young for me." Before Auntie Nessa could respond Vik was back with them. He stood next to Hadassah, lifting her gaze to meet his. He laughed before he spoke, "Girl, you look like a shiny raccoon. Go to your room and I'll send for you later. We're going to be gone for a couple of days. I just wanted you to meet who will be with you on the days Auntie Nessa can't go out."

"It's nice to meet you, Sean." She nodded in Derek's direction, then moved around the desk and leaned over to give Vik the customary kiss on the cheek. "I'll see you later."

Vik smiled and nodded his appreciation of the gesture. Hadassah stepped into the hallway and almost skipped back to her room. She was going home, soon. Taking deep breaths as she walked, replaying what her uncle said, free the girls. All of them. A miracle had just happened, but there were no angels delivering the message. Benny T had been a street dude his entire life. There would be no way to avoid a battle because Vik would not go down easy. The fight for her freedom was before her and she was more than ready.

She was lost in her thoughts when she made it to the door. It was cracked and she felt a breeze glide across the top of her feet. People were screaming and yelling. She could hear exactly what was going on outside, which was shocking because she had heard nothing from the outside with the barred window in place. It had never been opened.

Hadassah slowly turned the knob and stepped into the room. She grabbed her chest and leaned against the nearest wall. The window was open and the bar had been pushed up from the bottom right corner like the top on a sardine can.

Her heart raced; Sam's shoes were right under the windowsill. A piece of paper was fluttering on her roommate's bed.

"No, Sam. Please Sam, please tell me you didn't do this." Her blood curdling scream was enough to shake the building. She dropped on Sam's bed, snatched the note and held it to her chest.

She was screaming and rocking back and forth on the bed as every moment from the day she was snatched in the park came to the fore-front of her mind. The holding room. She screamed! Brittany being pregnant. She screamed! Shayla's bloody ponytail. She screamed! Vik taking her virginity. She screamed! She was still screaming when Auntie Nessa slapped her hard enough that she fell to the floor.

Turning her head and through blurry tears she found Vik, Sean and Benny T standing in the room. Auntie Nessa lifted Hadassah from the floor and walked her towards the door. "Come on baby, let them take care of this."

Hadassah crumpled the noted and stuffed it in her pocket. She was still crying as they left the room.

'He lied to me and used me. They will never let me go, today I am free.'

CHAPTER 21

Sean, Vik and Benny T were looking at each other as if deciding who was going to look out the window.

Vik leaned out first. He didn't say a word as he slumped against the wall and began loosening his tie.

Sean peered out next then turned back to Vik whose face was flushed. "Is she one of ours?"

Vik nodded a recognizable yes.

"Damn," Benny yelled. "We gotta get down there quick and get that body."

Vik straightened up, trying to compose himself. "Yes, get her before the police come."

The man was fighting to control himself. "Put her in the Escalade and we'll take care of it later. Hurry up!"

Benny signaled to Sean. "Let's go man, we gotta get down there and act like we're taking her to the hospital or something." He turned to leave with Sean following close behind.

When they made it to the first floor, Benny went through the front entrance and instructed Sean to go through a secret doorway that led to the residents exit. When Benny stepped through the door the faint sound of approaching sirens echoed with a sense of urgency.

Sean took a deep breath before stepping outside.   He wasn't sure what they could actually do with a bloody broken body in front of all these people, but he also couldn't blow his cover. Now that he had found Hadassah, he had to finish the three-fold mission; make sure Hadassah and the rest of the girls got out, bring Vik down and take down the cops and politicians who supported him. Having a dead body on the Towers property was going to bring heat that he hadn't planned on. No one at his precinct, outside of his Commander was aware of what he was doing and they would surely recognize him.

As soon as he stepped closer to the crowd, Benny T shook his head. He scanned the area and couldn't see the dead girl for the people crowding around her; some covered their mouths and some were crying. They were pointing upwards towards the building through their sobs and tears. No way they could pick up the corpse now. Benny T, walked over to him and whispered without moving his head.

"We need to get upstairs and get all the dates out of the building and lock all the girls in their rooms before they find out what happened." Sean nodded and they both rushed towards the building.

As they stepped through the door Sean heard a woman say, "She probably one of the girls working up there in that ho' house. They think don't nobody know about what they doing up there.' Another voice chimed in, "Yeah we see all those men in suits coming in that black truck; coming and going all times of the day and night like they having business meetings."

People in the crowd agreed with her as Benny T shut and dead bolted the door.

Sean followed Benny T to the service elevator that was used for the clients connected to the Bayou. Along with the walls and staircases being reconstructed, a door was cut into the brick on the south side of the building which served as another entrance to the Bayou.

Sean turned to Benny T. "What do we do now? This is Federally funded property, so I know we're about to have the police and people from the housing swarming around. Not to mention the Feds."

With one hand in his pocket on the weapon he held there, and the other hand rubbed across his chin, he seemed to be in a trance as he spoke. "Yeah, looks like ol' Vik's time is finally up."   Before Sean could ask what, he meant by that statement the elevator door opened and they were off shut the Bayou down and report to Vik.

Vik was moving slowly about his office in silence. When he looked up at the two men entering the room, he tried to maintain his composure. "Where have you guys been, what took you so long and where's Sam's body?"

Benny spoke first. "Vik, we couldn't get the body. There were too many people standing around. We hurried up and got all the dates out so we could focus on our next move."

Vik froze, his head whipped to Sean. "What does he mean you couldn't get the body?"

"There were too many people standing around her." Benny repeated, talking loud with flailing hands. "People yelling, screaming, crying, the ambulance and police were coming. There was no way we could have just picked up a dead body and brought it into the building or put it in the truck."

"All right, All right." Silence following that admission was unnerving. Vik said, as he gathered papers from his desk and dropped them in an open briefcase.

"Good thinking that you got all the dates out. I need to get over to building one with Mr. Lattimore. I know the residents are all over his office."

He turned to face Hadassah as she sat motionless in the chair next to the window.

"Get a bag ready, when I come back up, you're still going with me tonight."

"Yes Vik," Hadassah said softly, and Sean wondered what that meant.

Just as she was stepping over the threshold Benny T turned to Vik and said,

"So, you ain't even gonna ask her how the bars got pulled back and the window open?"

Hadassah stopped dead in her tracks and turned to Benny T with an angry glare. "What do you mean by that?"

"Just what I said," he shot back. "You gonna stand here and tell us you don't know how she bent up a metal bar that was screwed into the wall and got the window open?"

Before she could answer Auntie Nessa walked up and nudged her back into the room, holding up something shiny. "This is how she got the screw out."

"What's that?" Sean asked peering at the item.

Auntie walked over and tossed the item onto Vik's desk.

"A broken finger nail file. A few weeks ago, I was giving some girls manicures and it broke. I threw it in the garbage and thought nothing of it."

"She must have been screwing it a little bit every day." She pulled a paper towel from her pocket that contained paint and drywall chips. "Found this in a hole cut in her mattress."

"You gotta be fu-! You gotta be kidding me." Benny turned to Hadassah again, "I'm going to ask you again trick, so y-."

"Watch your mouth, Benny." Vik looked Benny T square on. "Don't speak to her that way."

"What you in love now? Just because you the only one had her, you think she something special?"

In one motion Benny T lunged toward Hadassah with his hands reaching for her throat. Sean and Vik moved to grab him, but Sean made it to him first, locking his arms behind his back. Auntie Nessa had grabbed Hadassah, moving her out of his reach.

Benny T was trying to wrestle out of Sean's grip. Hadassah stepped from behind Auntie Nessa extracting the note from her pocket. The fury in her eyes was something Sean had never seen before.

"You know what? You're the reason she jumped." She handed Vik the note. "He was sleeping with her all the time, feeding her information and using her to keep tabs on everybody including you. Ain't that right Benny T?" she said in a slow calculated tone.

Benny's face froze in an expression that showed his shock. He looked at Vik who stared at him for several moments after he read the note.

"She's lying Vik," Benny yelled.

"Am I lying Benny T? How did she know everything about Brittany, Van and your plan to take over the Bayou. She had just told me and I was waiting to be alone with Vik to tell him."

Before she could say another word, Benny T lunged at her again breaking free from Sean's grip. Before Sean could get a hold of him, Hadassah's foot caught him in the groin.

"You black bitch," he yelped, grabbing his private parts. He was still reaching for her with his free hand when Sean cold cocked him in the jaw. His head slammed into Vik's desk, before he hit the floor, his breathing was shallow.

Vik stood over him shaking his head.

"Judas, right up under my nose. So, you had a plan to take me out?" Vik kicked Benny T in the side. "Me, you tried to take over what I've spent ten years building. I picked you up off the street. Pulled you out of that gang life. Gave you a job, status and this is how you repay me?"

He kicked him again hard in the ribs. The cracking sound that followed was unmistakable. He gestured towards Sean to grab Benny. "Get this trash out of my office and lock him up." Sean gripped Benny T and dragged him towards the door. "I have to get over to the office. Auntie Nessa make sure Hadassah stays with you. Lock everything down and wait for my call." He put one last look on the man who betrayed him. "Who's the trick now?"

Sean bent over, grabbed Benny T by his ankles and dragged him to the apartment across the hall. He took his keys and his phone, locking the door behind him.

"I'll be back. You three go the kitchen until I call. Hadassah have your bag ready as soon as I come back." He grabbed her by the back of her neck, pulling her close then kissed her forehead. "As soon as we get this under control, I'm coming for you."

She nodded as he walked past with his briefcase.

"Alright, I'll lock up everything and be right here," Sean said as he moved behind Vik's desk and started straightening up the mess made in the scuffle. Auntie Nessa was shaking her head as she left mumbling something Sean couldn't make out.

A few minutes later, Hadassah peeked her head back in the room, and softly closed the door almost shut. "What do we do now? How are we all going to get out?"

"I don't know, "Derek responded. "I need to contact my Commander to put a tactical team in place around the building.

Hadassah went to the file cabinet and opened the first two drawers. "What are you doing?"

"Looking for the black book. That's where he keeps the names of all the dates." She pulled it from the back of the cabinet.

"This is it." She was smiling as she held the book with both hands for dear life.

He stepped over to her and hugged her tight. "You're on the money. But we can't take the book right now. Vik is gonna come back over here and be looking for it. He needs it to call in favors. Put it back and I'll try to get it before we all leave."

After he memorized a few names, she put the book back exactly where she found it and closed the drawer.

"Hurry and get your bag. We can't blow my cover. Just pay attention to everything I do and say. He's not about to give all this up."

Hadassah gave him one more quick hug. "I trust you." He pulled her arms down and squeezed his hands around hers.

"I got you baby girl, right now there's no time for this. This whole thing is about to blow up real quick."

"You're going to be the only one who can assist. I need you to focus and not move in any emotion. Leave now, I'll see you in the kitchen."

She remained in place.

Derek met Hadassah's teary eyes with a stern look. "I need you to focus. No feelings, only action. We got this, now hurry."

She sprang from the office. He hurried to finish straightening the desk and chairs so Auntie Nessa wouldn't come looking for him.

He turned off the light and locked the door, making a mental note of which drawer contained that book that would put everyone involved away for a long time.

CHAPTER 22

When Hadassah reached the kitchen Auntie Nessa was sipping from a whiskey glass. She chugged the brown liquid down in short gulps, making a sour face as she sat the glass down then picked up the half-smoked cigarette and puffed hard. Sean was already there, drinking a bottle of water, but watching Auntie Nessa closely.

Hadassah took a seat near the freezer. "So, what happens now? What's going to happen to Sam's body?"

"Well." Auntie Nessa said after another drag from the cigarette. "When she got here two years ago, she was a runaway. She was a tough cookie, a real hustler. Had the dates buying her all kinds of gifts; yeah, they always wanted Sam." She finished the liquor in the glass.

"Sam wanted to make her way to the top. She had no real family and had been in foster homes since she was five.

"Isn't that going to bring some heat?" Sean asked after tossing his bottle in the trash.

"I'm sure she's been listed as a missing person." He leaned against the back of the chair. "How do we protect the bayou?

Nessa nodded to his question then shrugged.

"We have to be expecting someone to come and try to figure out where she fell from," he persisted ignoring Auntie Nessa's warning glare.

Nessa poured herself another drink and lit another cigarette. "You got that right. The walls that separate the Bayou from everything else should keep them out for a minute, but we don't know for how long. The last time we had a problem, a girl got away before Benny T could get her back. They had to come up with a quick plan to throw off the authorities. Vik had planned on taking the girls to the Bayou down in Louisiana to his father's spot." She gulped half the liquor down hard.

Hadassah absorbed every word.

"His father's spot?" Sean asked with a quick look at Hadassah who shrugged.

Auntie Nessa took a long drag off the cigarette and watched the smoke disappear into the air. "Vik comes from pimp royalty. His daddy runs the biggest Gentleman's Club south of the Mason Dixon."

Hadassah's eyes widened with shock.

"His mama and daddy sent him to one of those fancy Black private colleges thinking that was going to save him." She chuckled.

"With all that schooling and political connections, there is nothing he wants more than the power his father has; Big Vik, that's what everybody calls him."

The liquor took effect as Nessa poured another drink and her words started dragging.

"He always talks about how his daddy never went further than the seventh grade, but the biggest names in the bible belt go to him for the best poontang in the South. There aren't girls anywhere more beautiful and well taken care of than Big Vik's girls. It's where men go for more than just sex."

She let out a snicker and laid her head against the wall. "They go there to cheat on their wives. They go when they're sad after their wives die. They take their sons when they think it's time for them to become a man."

This time she chuckled, and pointed a bent finger between them.

"Don't neither one of you ever forget, that all is fair in love and war and sometimes it's war. And I believe a war has been started."

She burped loud and covered her mouth. "Oopsie, 'scuse me y'all."

"Don't think this all gonna be over in one day." She stood up, placing her hands on the table to balance herself.

"If nobody was looking for that little girl before, someone is gonna be looking for her now." She picked up the bottle and the glass and headed toward her room. "Ol' Auntie Nessa might have to find someone else to take care of. Come get me when Vik comes in." She hummed as she swayed down the hallway.

Sean leaned towards Hadassah, checking to make sure Auntie Nessa had turned into her room and closed the door before he spoke. "We're gonna have to do something fast. If Vik takes those girls down to Louisiana, they might never make it back here."

These words struck a nerve of fear. "What am I supposed to do?" she whispered. "How are we supposed to make that happen? Some of these girls have been here for years and they like it, they may not even follow me out."

Derek was talking in a deep whisper. His niece looked at the intensity in his eyes and didn't move, speak or even blink. "Niece, whatever happens, you have to tell your story; not somebody else. You can come out of this and not live the rest of your life as a victim. You've already won, we're going home." He reached for her hands; then snatched them back after looking down the hall and towards the elevator. "Whoever wants to come can come, and whoever doesn't, that's on them. But I'm not leaving you. Go to your room and wait for Vik."

She stood and squeezed her uncle's arm before turning to leave.

CHAPTER 23

*S*ix hours had passed since Sam freed herself from the jaws of the Bayou. Vik had to stay while police and investigators questioned him along with the residents and people in the neighborhood.

Vik nudged Sean who had fallen asleep on the thick wooden table with his head on crossed arms. "Get up, let's go deal with Benny T. He's the cause of all this commotion. We're about to get some answers."

Sean stretched and followed him to the room. When he opened the door Benny T was sitting on the floor against the wall, smiling as they came in.

"So now what, Vik?" he questioned. "You gonna turn on me for this new dude and that trick you done fell in love with?" Benny T was in full street mode. He wasn't holding back on words or anything else. Vik walked over to him and snatched him by the collar until their faces met. "You're the reason all this happened. There's police crawling all over this place. Whatever you did or said to that girl to make her jump out the window is the evil that's in you." He pulled the collar tighter, nearly lifting the man off the ground. "We have a $50,000 a week operation here and now all that's down the drain because you couldn't keep your dick in your pants and was selling that little girl a pipe dream. You think we can sweep this under the rug like we did when the last girl got away?" Benny T never looked away and the smile never left his face

"We have a dead body on our property. A dead girl that's been missing for two years and now the Feds want to know where she's been and how she fell from an eight-story window." He pushed him hard against the wall.

Benny T straightened his collar and laughed out loud. "I ain't tell that trick nothing but the truth," he said. "I was gunning for you and your precious Dark and Lovely. I've wanted that ass since she got here, but you made sure you got to her first."

Vik punched Benny T hard in the mouth, loosening his tooth. Sean was glad he did it first. It took everything not to bash his head in after what he said about Hadassah.

The blow nor the blood phased him at all.

"Man are you that proper, dumb and blind. You're so smart 'til you're stupid." Sean stepped up; punching him in the stomach so he folded over.

"You can beat me, torture me, it ain't gonna matter. They're coming for you." He was still bent over holding his stomach, slobbering and laughing at the same time. "You're the trick now. You think they voted you back in because they like you. You think they want to promote you up higher because you're the man?", he screamed.

"They want this, all of it and they're gonna get it." "You're the trick Vik." He wiped slob from his mouth and stood tall. His voice now louder. "They want you out because you got dirt on them. You think they don't know about your black book? All the tricks talk."

"They all know about the Bayou and you're going down. That trick jumping out the window just gave them the in they needed." He pointed at Vik, his body was shaking violently as the veins in his neck protruded. "You won't be able to make another move or another dollar." He reared back on his heels and threw his head back, laughing. "You're finished pretty, proper boy." Sean stepped towards Benny T again, this time Vik stopped him.

"Friggin' Judas. My father always said, your closest friend is your closest enemy." Vik smoothed out the front of his suit. "I built this. This is my empire and no one, not a soul is taking it from me. I'll burn it to the ground before I hand it over." Vik grabbed Benny T by his head and brought his knee up to his nose. The bone cracked but he didn't flinch. Benny T let out a yelp and went down, blood oozing through his fingers that cuffed his face.

"This explains why you've been picking with Hadassah this whole time. You wanted her for yourself you grimy bastard."

Vik focused on Sean as he said, "I need to call my people. I'm going to have someone come get this traitor and we need to plan to move the girls early in the morning. The police will be back with the Feds tomorrow and the investigation won't end until they have answers. Today they're focused on finding out who Sam is and contacting people who knew her. We don't have any time." Sean followed him from the room, locking the door again on Benny T. Vik turned to him.

"Hey Sean, I know you're new to all this, but I want you to know I appreciate you." He touched Sean's shoulder. Sean smiled, but inside he wanted to choke the man standing before him, that had caused so much harm and was now needed his help.

"You've come through in a short time and I'm grateful for you man." He tapped his shoulder.

"I need to know you're with me all the way. It might mean not going back to the half-way house and violating your probation. But I swear, you'll be taken care of once we get to Louisiana. Once this blows over, I'll call in a favor and straighten things out for you." Sean pretended to give it some thought before saying, "I'm with you Vik."

Vik was looking him square in the face and the relief was clear. "Good, I'm going to make these calls, we need a couple of vans, we can't take any chances putting all the girls in the minibus. Everybody's going to be watching every move we make now. You take Hadassah and get the girls packed and ready. Let them all know to only bring one bag. We have to travel light, with only two vans and a long ride to the south."

Sean mulled a few things over. His chances of saving his niece and the rest of the girls was waning if they left.

"I got it covered, Vik the girls will be ready to move whenever you say." He paused. "Let me ask you a question though."

Vik raised an eyebrow. "What is it?"

Sean rubbed his chin. "What do you think about taking them out the side door tonight and staying in a motel, maybe somewhere on Roosevelt?" We can't just get seventeen girls and Auntie Nessa out first thing in the morning. Someone is bound to see that type of movement."

Vik paced the floor a few moments.

"Good thinking. Okay, let me pull this transportation together so we can move the girls when this neighborhood is the quietest."

He dabbed Sean on the arm before walking towards his office, glancing over his shoulder without breaking his stride.

"We've got a long ride to New Orleans."

"Got it." Sean shot back. He needed to talk to Hadassah quick before they went to get

the girls ready. He hadn't been able to get word to his Commander to prepare the special assignment team. Derek could only pray none of the officers were on Vik's payroll. Sean needed a plan quick; time was running out and he was still aiming to maintain his cover.

CHAPTER 24

*R*ight after Sam jumped, Vik called four of his cousins to provide reinforcement letting them know to be on standby while he waited for Sean and Benny T to take care of Sam's body.

"I don't have everything hashed out, but I know two things. We need to dispose of Benny T and get the girls to my father's place in New Orleans."

"I'll have to make sure everything in the front office is clear and ready for more investigating tomorrow." Sean nodded as he took it all in and could tell Vik was unraveling by going back and forth to Mr. Lattimore's office and take care of the Bayou at the same time.

Most of Vik's cousins lived in New Orleans, about fifteen minutes from his parents' estate in Metairie, Louisiana, but Big Vik had moved some relatives into a home just North of Chicago to be at his son's disposal if ever needed; like now.

"Listen." He spoke to his cousins via facetime with Sean standing in the background. Sean tried to get a look at their faces, to commit them to memory in case anyone tried to get away.

According to Vik, his cousins Nero, Tiny, Chico and Al would make it to the Towers within thirty minutes.

"Hey Vik, I'm going outside for a minute and see what's happening"

"Okay, come right back. The vans will be here soon," Vik mumbled before turning back to his phone.

Sean spent about twenty minutes in the courtyard to get the temperature of what was happening and was able to contact his Commander.

* * *

"So did you find out anything?" Vik questioned as he moved about the office sliding papers in his briefcase.

"The police have been talking to everyone in the Towers including people that are in the Circle every day. Some of them told the police about Benny T and the Escalade."

"All the more reason for us to get out of here soon as its dark enough."

"I'm ready," Sean stated, then took a deep breath and readied himself for the battle that laid ahead. This seemed to be his last chance to put a stop to everything. He couldn't have any missteps.

"The crime scene investigators are still trying to figure out the exact location she jumped from. Mr. Lattimore told me that one of the agents called the city clerk and requested the blueprint of the building's layout. They will find the Bayou by this time tomorrow."

Vik picked up the phone on his desk and dialed. "Mr. Lattimore, I need you to stall the authorities for a couple of days until I make it back from Louisiana," He paused for a moment, listening. "I know you'll do your best." Vik placed the phone in the cradle and continued packing his briefcase. "I have to go back to Lattimore's office one more time before we leave. I have no idea how this is going to play out."

Neither do I. Sean thought to himself.

He stopped for a minute and sat down. Interlacing his hands behind his head as he rested against the thick leather chair. "I wonder how long Benny has been working against me and with who?"

Perching on the edge of the chair, Sean interrupted Vik's train of thought. "I'm just thinking about the time short time frame we're working with now, do you think a you should go back to Mr. Lattimore's sooner than later to see if we can at least shut that office down withing the next few hours?"

"Good thinking Sean. You're right. I need to make sure Lattimore keeps his cool. If the Bayou is discovered I'm facing charges of sex-trafficking, illegal conduct on Federally funded property, kidnapping and whatever other charges they throw at me." He let out a deep sigh, hands still behind his head. "Whoever's conspiring with Benny is ready to take it all."

The man was losing his grip and that was not good.

"Okay Vik I think your words confirm it." He said tapping lightly clenched fists."Go to the office, shut it down and let's get ready to get out of here."

Vik picked up his phone and swept from the office without looking back at Sean.

CHAPTER 25

*H*adassah tried to answer every question the girls had as they were rushing out of the building and loading into the vans. The windows on the vans were covered so no one could see in or out. That only increased their questioning because they had always traveled together in the mini-bus.

"Something's wrong," said Sophia one of the Latina girls. "Something's going on. They came in and stopped me in the middle of a date. Made the guy leave and took me to my room," she said as she took a seat.

One girl after another voiced their concerns. Hadassah just waited for her uncle.

"I wonder if this is going to be like the last time." This query came from Cheyenne, a red-haired Caucasian girl with hazel eyes, who angled in her seat to face Sophia.

"Remember when they were going to take us to Louisiana after Kelly got away?"

"Look, everything is going to be okay." Hadassah was standing next to the driver as she put a steadying grip on the back of the first seat.

Sophia stood peering at Hadassah. "How do you know everything is going to be okay? There are some strange things going today and nobody has said anything."

Before she could say another word, Lily spoke up. "You got that right. Did you notice Benny T wasn't with us when we came downstairs?" Murmurs of discontent arose from the rest of the girls.

Sophia pointed a loose finger in the air. "And guess who else wasn't with us, Sam?" Now all then girls in the van were searching the faces of those around them. Some had fearful expressions, while others had ones of curiosity or irritation.

"I know everything is going to be okay, because I said so." She cut her eyes and nodded towards the driver while trying not to draw his attention. Hadassah motioned for everyone to simmer down.

Sophia gave her a smile that signaled she understood Hadassah's movements. "Okay, Ms. Hadassah, we'll sit down and see what happens." Sophia winked at Lilly who had kept her focus on the other vocal one. Hadassah saw Lilly nod then turn to the front of the van.

Hadassah stepped out and found the girls in the other van were just as curious, but not as vocal as Sophia and Lilly. Everyone had the same question 'where were they going?' but she couldn't tell them what she knew.

She moved back and forth between the vans parked one behind the other right next to the side door. What could be taking Vik, Auntie Nessa and Sean so long to come downstairs? There was the same tug of uneasiness in her stomach she felt right before Benny T said he was taking Sam upstairs for her next date; right before she jumped.

She tapped her hand against her leg like she always did when she was nervous as several thoughts bounced around in her head.

Her uncle hadn't given her a solid plan yet, and they were running out of time.

Vik said his main concern was getting the girls off the property.

Hadassah tried to figure out how she was going to get the girls to be a part of their own rescue. The only chance they had to get away would be at the motel, whether her uncle helped or not. If they drew enough attention, somebody was bound to call the police. Anyone working with Vik would have a gun, so she had to be intentional with any moves she made so that no one else died.

The driver of the second van, Vik's cousin Nero, was loudly tapping his foot.

Then he tapped the steering wheel, all while he huffed and puffed. "We need to see what's going on," he growled. "I'm not about to be caught up. Why is it taking us so long to move?"

"I don't know, just chill. They're coming," Hadassah answered.

She hoped everything would get in motion quick. The girls and both drivers were going to cause problems if they kept sitting there.

She hadn't been told the plan for Benny T, but she did know he wasn't going with them. As far as she knew, he was still locked in the apartment across from Vik's office.

Hadassah had only been outside Chicago a few times, and never out of Illinois. After the death of her parents, Uncle Derek, Mama Betty and Uncle Louis kept her extremely close.

What would happen if they were all taken down to Louisiana before Uncle Derek's team could rescue them? Would she ever make it back to Chicago and see her family?

Had Uncle Derek ever gotten the chance to communicate to her grandmother that he had found her?

The driver of the van which was parked closest to the door interrupted her thoughts.

"Hey, we need to get moving if we want to clear out of here before day break. We don't want to draw any attention going into a motel with twenty something people." She glanced over her shoulder to the entrance. Still nothing.

"Can you run up and see what's the hold up?" His thick French accent, similar to Vik's made Hadassah think he was also from New Orleans.

"I'll go check." She told the girls in both vans to sit tight and she'd be right back. Some of the girls were angry, restless and grumbling. The short distance from the vans back to the side door seemed like a mile as the growing pit in her stomach made her feet feel as though she was lifting steel with each step.

Just as she made it through the side door, the freight elevator closed. "Dang it." she mumbled to herself. Viktor's no profanity policy had quickly become her habit. She wasn't that much of a curser, anyway. Her uncle Derek said women who cursed a lot had a small vocabulary. As beautifully as Auntie Nessa had decorated the freight elevator, to make it more comfortable for the dates, it still moved at a snail's pace. She didn't feel like trekking up the nine flights but there wasn't much choice.

She tapped a hand against her leg. She couldn't put her finger on it, but a tight ball was forming in the pit of her stomach.

CHAPTER 26

$\mathcal{A}$untie Nessa stood a few from the freight elevator with supplies in hand. She had packed everything she thought she needed and got the space cleared for Vik and Mr. Lattimore to seal up both floors of the Bayou. Two bags with long straps were pulled across her chest and shoulders, and what looked like two medical bags; one in each hand.

Vik's cousin Chico was sent up to help Sean dispose of Benny T, while Al and Nero both waited in the vans. Benny T was wearing he usual sinister smile as he stood held between Sean and Chico, his wrists held together by a thin zip-tie.

"Y'all think it's gonna be easy to get rid of me? We'll see." Benny T had coughed, broke free from the zip-tie and suddenly elbowed Chico in the bridge of his nose. "Ah, damn," Chico yelped falling to the floor while grabbing his face; blinded by the gushing blood. Benny lunged toward the floor breaking free from Sean's grasp with a dive at Nessa's ankles, pulling her to the floor. Sean tried to grab Benny's leg but he kicked him in the shoulder hard. Before Sean could reach for him again, Benny caught his forehead with the heel of his shoe. Sean had lost strength from the force of the last kick.

"Get off me you bastard," Nessa shouted. She couldn't get her bearings because her arms were entangled in the straps of the bags.

"Shut up, you sissy." Benny landed two quick punches in Nessa's face leaving her dazed. He ripped her shirt and snatched the switchblade from her bra and stood with his usual wicked grin, yielding the weapon, armed for battle.

Sean was now on his knees about to make a move towards Benny when Hadassah sprung through the elevator door. Benny grabbed her, wrapping his arm around her neck like an irritated python as he held the switchblade next to her ear.

Chico was still howling on the floor in a fetal position, blood oozing through his hands.

"Everybody, stay down. If anybody moves, I'm slicing this black wench's throat and I mean it."

"And you, Dark and Lovely, are coming with *me* tonight."

Hadassah was trying to break free from his grasp while looking to her uncle for help her tussling making Benny squeeze tighter. "Be still or I'll break your damn neck," he snarled, then licked the side of her face from her bottom jawbone up to her eyebrow. "I've been wanting this ass and tonight I'm gonna get it."

Sean had to make a split-second decision with his next move keeping Hadassah as his first priority. He looked her directly in the eyes and put his head down, three blinks as a count. Hadassah put all her weight into dropping her small frame to the floor. Tiny snuck up behind Benny T from the kitchen's side door. As Benny tried to pull Hadassah to her feet, Tiny slammed him in the head with the butt of the gun. Benny let out a loud cry. "You mutha-." He released Hadassah, grabbing his head, bending towards the floor. Tiny stepped to Benny to strike again. "Argh" he yelled falling against the wall as the switchblade dug deep into his lungs as the gun clattered to the floor.

Benny quickly scrambled for the weapon; in a single motion he was on one knee, aimed towards Hadassah pulling the trigger before Sean could stop him. Everything happened so fast; Hadassah didn't know what to do. Auntie Nessa screamed "NO!"

The gun blasted in her ears and a sudden heaviness slammed

against her body knocking her to the floor. She could barely breathe as the weight became heavier.

Sean finally pulled his service gun; he had brought it along against his Commander's orders. He fired the 9mm catching Benny in the middle of his chest.

Benny's body fell hard against the wall, then plummeted face down on the hardwood floor.

Hadassah was struggling, still pinned under Auntie Nessa's massive body.

"Are you hurt? Sean asked "where's the blood coming from? Are you hit?"

 "No, no I'm okay." She maneuvered until she could kneel next to Auntie Nessa who was gasping for air. Blood gushed from the wound and her mouth.

"Auntie, Auntie, no, please Auntie." Hadassah screamed.

Auntie Nessa reached up, gently touching Hadassah's face. "Dark, yet she is lovely." She gasped for the next breath. "Make sure everyone goes free."

Her limp hand fell to the floor and her eyes closed.

Sean pulled Hadassah up. "Come on, we have to get out before Vik comes back."

"Before Vik comes back and what?" Vik was now standing before them with Nero at his side, both of them looking a bit winded from the trek up the nine flights of stairs.

"How did all this happen this fast? Nero help Chico up."

Hadassah was leaning against the wall near Nessa's body, crying hysterically.

Sean tucked his service gun away in a holster on his ankle then picked up Tiny's gun on the sly.

"Everything got outta hand real quick," Sean was speaking through rushed breaths. We were waiting for the elevator and Benny T went crazy. He broke Chico's nose, tried to kidnap Hadassah and then tried to shoot her, killing Nessa instead. He was like a madman. I had to put him down."

Vik shook his head as he walked to Hadassah, pulling her into his chest.

"I'm okay," she whispered through tears after a few seconds". "I'm just shook up, everything happened so fast. Benny tried to kill me and Auntie Nessa jumped in the way." She lowered her head against his chest, still crying. Vik stroked the back of her hair.

"It's okay, we're about to get out of here. Once we get to my dad's place, we'll be okay." He scanned the scene, taking in the bodies. "Go see if you can find something for Chico's face. We'll have to take care of these others later."

"You all need to hurry. Me and Nero will be right behind you. Al knows the motel where we're all going to meet up. Sean, you're going to have to drive one of the vans now. I'm gonna need Nero to call in some people to help clean this up before the Feds get up here." He gently squeezed Hadassah's shoulder, as she walked past him taking the towel to Chico, then turned to Sean. "Are you okay? Have you ever shot anybody before now?" He was looking at Benny's body, disgust in his expression.

"Let's just say, this is not the first time I did what I had to do." He was looking at Vik eye-to-eye.

Vik held out a lightly clenched fist towards Sean and Sean returned the gesture giving him a knuckle-to-knuckle fist bump.

"Thank you for protecting Hadassah. I don't know what I would've done if I came up here and she was dead."

Sean nodded as Vik took another deep breath.

"Let's move out."

He pressed the button for the elevator.

"Keep that towel pressed against your face," he said pointing to Chico. "We'll get it looked at once we make it to the motel. We have to hurry; the sun is coming up."

Hadassah assisted Chico with walking to the elevator.

Sean kept a straight face as they all leaned against the elevator wall all while Hadassah was trying to keep herself together.

He breathed a sigh of relief when the elevator doors shut.

CHAPTER 27

*V*ik had lost two of his small crew within minutes and Sean needed to update his Commander on which motel they were going to before the vans got on the highway. He was proud of his niece and how she explained that Al had sent her upstairs to find out what was taking so long. She had kept her composure and didn't blow his cover at the last minute. Freedom was too close for everyone.

As the elevator descended floor to floor, Hadassah opened her mouth to speak. Sean slightly shook his head, glancing at Chico, who was still trying to recover, from what was probably a broken nose.

"Damn, what happened?" Al asked, as Sean helped Chico into the van and instructed the two girls in the first seat to move over for the injured young man to take the spot. "Ming, I need you to keep applying pressure with this towel until the bleeding stops."

She nodded and reached for the bloody towel. Chico winced when the towel was pressed against his nose.

"I know it hurts man, but we have to stop the bleeding. Vik's going to send someone to the motel as soon as we get there."

"Make sure he doesn't lose consciousness," Sean warned.

"Okay Sean, I got it," Ming said, "If nothing else, I know how to take care of a man." They all laughed a light laugh. It had been a while since Sean had even smiled.

"Okay Al, you lead the way. Vik said you know the motel we're going to."

"Finally. The sun's coming up, we're already behind the ball." He started the engine. "As soon as you get in the driver's seat we need to pull off."

"Alright man, I'm ready." Sean gave everyone a nod. "Everything's going to be okay ladies. We had a slight hiccup, but we're fine now." He tried to smile, but it wasn't with any confidence. Thanks to Benny T, his plan had already gone sideways.

"Y'all keep saying everything is okay," a tall dark-haired Brazilian girl said from her seat a few rows behind Chico and Ming. "But nobody has said what's wrong." She huffed and laid her head against the seat.

"Give us time." Sean stepped down and walked to the second van where Hadassah was doing her best to calm all the girls down.

"Why is there blood on your shirt? What happened up there? You were only up there like fifteen minutes." Sophia said. She stood and looked over Hadassah's shoulder. "And where is Auntie Nessa?"

Hadassah froze. The image of Nessa's body bleeding on the floor flashed in her head. She choked back a sob before she said, "Getting everybody worked up isn't going to help the situation. We have to go and that's it. Auntie Nessa will catch up with us at the motel." The lie slipped easily from her lips. As she moved into the seat next to a Jamaican girl name Paige, who hadn't said a word the entire time, but was watching every move that everyone made.

Just as Sean stepped up into the van, he went back down. "I gotta take a quick leak before we pull off. I'll be right back." Before anyone could protest. He went to the back of the van and five minutes, later, he stepped into the van and sat in the driver's seat. The door was still closing as he pulled off, following Al.

Both vans pulled from the side of the building onto California Avenue, heading south towards Roosevelt Road. Just as the second van Sean was driving passed under the viaduct the back right tire started wobbling. Before he could pull over and check the issue, he hit a pothole, and the tire busted, sending it into a fishtail with the weight of eleven people dragging it along.

Screams went in the air. Luckily, they coasted through the light on Roosevelt right into the split of Douglas Park. If he made it into the park and hopped a curb, the grass would slow them down.

"Hold on everybody," he yelled. As soon as they made it to the left of the split he yelled. "Everybody grab your seatbelts or grab a seat real ti-."

Before he could finish his sentence, the van jumped the curb knocking off the entire rim and slid through the early morning dew coating the grass. Sean's foot never left the break. The van coasted a few feet and stopped right before the sidewalk separating the patch of grass from the lagoon.

He threw the van in park, and scanned the van row by row attempting to calm the girls, who were crying and yelling hysterically. "Is everybody okay?"

Hadassah was moving from seat to seat checking on everyone. "Is anyone hurt? Take some deep breaths?"

When they all calmed down, Sean went back to the driver's seat and scanned the area for the other van. Using a burner phone he got from one of the cigarette customers in the circle, he called Al.

"Turn around and come back for us. You didn't see what happened behind you? Dude we almost crashed."

Sean was sitting with his head against the driver's window as he spoke, with his free hand on his neatly tapered haircut. This tire incident would buy them some more time. The Commander was on standby for his next move once he had the motel name from Al. He had to play it all the way to the end. "Yeah man, I don't know what happened, the tire blew out." He paused as Al yelled obscenities between his questions.

"Al, I don't know how the rim came off, probably because the tire blew out. Dude, can you just come get us?"

He moved the phone away from his ear as Al screamed through the receiver.

"Look man, all that yelling ain't going to solve not-." Sean threw his head back in frustration as Al continued his tirade.

"Al, Al, please man, we don't have time for all this. Come get us and we're gonna have to just deal with us being squeezed in tight until we get to the motel. How far is the spot from here, anyway?" Al screamed the motel's name and location then disconnected the call.

Sean hung up, breathed a sigh of relief and relaxed against the back of the seat. He turned his head to the right to find Hadassah staring at him with an anxious look. He winked at her and closed his eyes. The one thing he would have to worry about is how to stay out of sight as much as possible when the other officers got there so his cover wouldn't be blown.

CHAPTER 28

"Look, we have to get out of here before people start noticing." Sean was trying to contain his irritation with Al's non-stop questioning. "The sun's almost up. You got something to take the plates off before I check the van to make sure we didn't leave anything?" Sean moved back to the empty van, did a quick sweep, then quickly removed the front and back plates. He climbed into the van, searching for a seat but the only available spot was the step where he stood. The girls had filled in every nook and cranny, including the floor.

Vik had secured two rooms at a flea bag motel near Roosevelt Road and Cicero Ave. Al split the girls up putting Sean with ten and the other seven with him and Chico, which included Hadassah. He had tried to keep Hadassah with him, but didn't want to raise any suspicion.

"Yeah, wassup man?" Sean was yawning and stretching from a light nap when Al knocked on the door. "I'm about to walk down the street to the lil' truck stop I saw as we were pulling into the lot and get everybody some breakfast." He was pointing in the direction of a flashing sign.

Sean stepped from the room closing the door behind him. "Al, are you crazy? In case you forgot, we have seventeen girls that we've been holding hostage. Do you really believe, you're gonna leave them and no one tries to escape?"

"Man, these hoes ain't going nowhere. Big Vik trained Vik B since he was a boy on how to work their minds. All these broads have Stockholm syndrome. Some of them believe Vik B, rescued them." He took a long drag off his cigarette, leaned against the rail and crossed his arms.

"I don't care what you're talking about, no one gets away. Stay here and send Hadassah. She's Vik's main girl. She's the one we don't have to worry about."

"Man, now you're the one talking crazy. She was a virgin when Vik snatched her. She's the main one who's gon' try to get away. She ain't even been here ninety days."

"Look man, it's my call. Give her the money and show her where the spot is."

"It's your ass if she gets away." He protested. "Tell her to come here."

Sean opened the door, calling for her. Some of the girls were asleep on the bed and the floor, some were watching the television. Hadassah walked out and Al handed her two hundred-dollars and pointed to the right. "See that sign blinking right there?"

She nodded.

"Take this money and get everybody a breakfast sandwich. When you get back stop downstairs at the convenience store and get some waters and juices."

She gave Sean a nervous look.

"If you even think about running, talking or letting anybody know what's going on." He tapped the gun in his front pocket. "You'll have to deal with me first."

"And after me, you'll have Vik to deal with and I know you don't want that."

She shook her head. "I won't do anything like that."

She placed the money in her bra and started down the metal and concrete stairs.

"She's cool man, you ain't gotta do all that." Sean said hitting Al on the shoulder.

"She better be." He stomped out the cigarette and went back to the room.

Sean placed both hands on the rail as he watched his niece cross the street. He had nothing but the hope that everything he had been teaching her since her parents died would pay off in this moment. Even at such an early hour the corner was buzzing. Passengers were waiting at all four bus stops. Customers were at the gas pumps of the station below them and there were several people walking up and down Cicero. This provided more than enough opportunity to draw some attention. They were going to hit the road as soon as nightfall came.

This was their last chance at a rescue before leaving Chicago and traveling to Louisiana, he was banking on his commander to show up with a rescue team.

CHAPTER 29

*H*adassah had lived on the southeast side of Chicago her entire life and had no clue where she was at the moment. The street signs here were the same. She scanned the Shell gas station, liquor store, factory and wholesale furniture store on each corner of the intersection of Roosevelt Road and Cicero Avenue. She locked in the names of each business she passed in the short distance from the motel. The truck stop smelled like old bacon and cigarette smoke. A few old men were laughing and talking loud in one of the corners. Brown tables took up the space between old, green leather booths; some being held together by black or grey tape.

"Hey baby, good morning. Whatchu' ordering today?" asked the middle-aged white woman with several missing teeth.

The cook working the grill behind the register heard her order for twenty bacon egg and cheese sandwiches on wheat toast. He turned to her with a wide gap-toothed grin.

"What the hell? Ya'll on a picnic or something? He mumbled. "Let me get this damn bacon going."

"Could you make that turkey bacon?" she asked softly to the cook glaring at her.

"Aw, damn." He snapped. "Now you want something special?"

"You ol' fool, fix the sandwiches," the waitress said "She's paying for them." The cook and the cashier broke into unified laughter.

The cashier plucked the money from Hadassah's manicured hand and asked her to take a seat on one of the worn black leather barstools that were also taped with the same gray tape in the booths.

"It'll be a minute; you want some coffee?"

"Sure, some coffee would be great." Hadassah gave her a weak smile.

"Don't worry, the coffee is on the house since you're buying so many sandwiches."

"Okay, thank you." Hadassah muffled.

She poured cream and sugar in the coffee like she saw her grandma do every morning when she would stay the night with her. She kept looking over her shoulder in fear of Al or Vik suddenly showing up as she stirred the coffee and took a few sips.

A thin white girl with stringy blonde hair strolled in and sat two spaces from Hadassah. She couldn't help but stare at the woman's black eye that she failed in trying to cover with make- up. "Whatchu' looking at? You ain't neva' seen nobody with a black eye?" she barked.

"Tina leave that girl alone, hell if I didn't know any better, I would be looking at you too."

The woman stuck her middle finger up at the cashier. "Hurry up and fix me a bowl of grits real quick. I gotta get back to work before Frankie comes through here." Hadassah had found something else to focus on.

She didn't know what she could do to let someone know she was in trouble. She tried to think of what her uncle would do if he was in this situation.

Hadassah was lost in her thoughts when the cashier spoke to her.

"Honey, your order is ready."

Hadassah reached for the bags; as she was standing, she intentionally knocked the almost full cup of coffee to the floor. "I'm sorry, I'll help you get it up."

"No, no honey, it's alright, I can clean this up in no time."

Hadassah had already pulled a hand full of napkins from the dispenser and was down on the floor wiping up the coffee making sure she was out of the line of sight for anyone watching from the motel.

The cashier grabbed some napkins too and bent down to help her. "I need you to call the thirty-ninth precinct" she whispered. "Ask for Commander Reid. Tell him badge number 0407 needs assistance at the Lazy Inn motel right down the street. We're in rooms 210 and 211."

"Wait, slow down a little, repeat that?" The cashier wrote the information on her green and white pad she used to take orders. "Okay got it."

Hadassah stood to leave, handing the cashier the soiled napkins. "Thank you, sorry again for spilling the coffee."

With food in tow, she hurried back to the motel stopping to get the drinks Al had ordered and went straight back to the rooms.

She knocked on the door of the adjacent room giving Sean enough sandwiches for him and the girls and passed out the sandwiches to the girls in the room with her who were awake. Almost all of them removed the bacon even though it was turkey. Auntie Nessa had converted most of them to a vegan and vegetarian diet. She answered all the questions she could and did her best to comfort the girls. They laughed and talked until each of them drifted off to sleep; it was now late afternoon. Even Al had surrendered to rest as he nestled in the chair next to the night stand. Chico had moved only once the entire time after Al had given him a double dose of over-the-counter pain relievers. *When was Vik coming?*

She could only hope that the cashier would follow through, she couldn't be sure they would make it in time. Would she be able to get the girls to help her? When her thoughts surrendered, she could feel herself and her eyelids began to drift into sleep.

A light knock on the door startled her; she opened her eyes, but her body didn't move.

"Everything all right in here?" Hadassah lifted her head when she heard her uncle's voice.

"Man, go back to your spot. I got this Al grumbled, rubbing his hands across his low haircut. Derek could see Hadassah smiling as he looked past Al to where she was on the bed.

"Everything's fine." Hadassah's lips curled into a slight grin. "It's fine now."

CHAPTER 30

$\mathcal{M}$r. Lattimore and Vik were horrified as they sat across the street watching the chaos unfold. The back doors of both vans were open and some of the windows were busted. Sophia and Lilly each had a crowbar and were breaking out the tinted windows on the side of one of the vans.

Al was lying at the bottom of the stairs not moving at all while three girls viciously kicked and stomped him.

"Damn Vik. What should we do?" Lattimore's face was filled with questions. "I've never seen the girls act like this."

"We're not going to do anything." He glanced in the rearview mirror.

Vik, who was sitting in the passenger seat, watched Ming, Brazilian Red and Tina pushing and pulling the big green dumpster that Sean was using for cover. Hadassah suddenly appeared and said something to the girls. Her hands were up as though she was trying to stop them.

Some of the girls were standing outside the doors of the motel rooms throwing everything from the bags they had all brought with them. While the remaining girls stood by the entrance of the convenience store crying as they huddled together; Chico was sitting on the stoop to the store's entrance, with a bloody towel against his face.

People were everywhere with their phones out recording and cheering the mob action of the girls.

"We definitely can't get out here."

A SWAT truck pulled up and men in black jumped out in tactical gear with weapons drawn to get the scene under control. From their position in the truck, with the windows down, both Vik and Lattimore could hear the officers' yelling commands to everyone in the parking lot.

Twenty minutes passed before all the girls and Sean were loaded into a paddy wagon. Al and Chico were taken away in ambulances.

When the last police vehicle pulled off Lattimore turned to Vik. "What if one of them talks? We can all be tied to the Bayou. I have a wife and kids; I can't go down like this."

Vik was staring straight ahead. "What the hell happened here today? The girls haven't even been here for twenty-four hours. How did they all just decide to rise up and fight?" He still didn't look at this partner. "Now, the police are taking most of them to the station. How did a SWAT team know to come here? Somebody had to drop a dime." He was tapping the dashboard one finger at a time.

"We have to go and see what's going on. Someone besides Benny betrayed me." Lattimore checked his phone, then back to the chaos.

"I can't even tell if anyone's missing. Tomorrow is day three since Sam died, the girls have been found, which means the authorities are not going to wait until tomorrow. They'll be back to the Towers today. They're probably already there." Vik was still staring straight ahead.

"The Feds are going to shut down all three buildings of the Towers, Vik," Lattimore continued.

"We're dead, we're caught boss, what do we do?" Lattimore was speaking in growing hysteria.

"Get out." Vik commanded.

"Get out, what do you mean, get out?" Lattimore now hysterical. Vik remained eerily calm.

"Go home to your wife and kids, take a shower, and go to work. It's still early. You could make it there by the afternoon. I'll contact you when I need you. Go to work and deal with whatever questions the Feds have. You can do it. I have faith in you."

"Vik, I can't jus-."

"Yes you can." Vik opened the door and walked to the driver's side and waited for Lattimore to exit the vehicle.

"Call an Uber or somebody. Go home to your family, change clothes and go to the building. I'll be in the office tomorrow." Vik instructed.

"Where are you going Vik? What time are you coming in tomorrow?"

Vik stepped around him and climbed back into the Escalade before closing the door.

"Everything will be worked out by this time tomorrow. I promise. Go home."

He peeled off, leaving Lattimore looking after him.

CHAPTER 31

"*I*s everyone out?" Did you knock on every door and check every apartment?" The fire chief asked the team."

"Yes sir, although the alarms on every floor were pulled," one of the fire fighters reported, "We have no evidence of smoke or a fire."

An explosion coming from the back of the third building caused everyone on the scene to clamor behind cars and trucks seeking the only shelter available.

The fire chief got on the radio, "All team members move to building three."

The red and orange flames lit up the dark morning sky.

Before the fire chief could follow, the voice of a child speaking to his mother pulled his attention. He took off his helmet, stepping over to them.

"Excuse me ma'am. I heard your son telling you about something he saw. Do you mind if I ask him a few questions?"

The woman, clad in a black bonnet, pink house coat and red crocs used her arm, gesturing the chief towards her son. "Go head, Terrell, tell him what you told me. I'm not gonna get you for sneaking in the hallway playing the game."

The small boy with dark sandy-hair and ivory skin looked at his mother and grabbed her hand, looking up to her.

"It's okay, I'm gonna let you slide this time."

The child was initially stammering when he started, but his voice cleared up and became stronger as he held onto his mother's hand.

"I had snuck in the hallway to play my Switch and I was sitting right by the door, so if my mama came, I could just close the door and jump in the chair."

The fireman knelt down so he and the child were face to face.

"A man came through the stairway. He had on all black and a black ski mask. He put his finger up to his mouth, like he was telling me to be quiet, then he pulled the fire alarm and went back to the stairway. That's when I ran in the house and told my mama 'nem it was a fire and we needed to get out fast."

"You say *he* had on a ski mask?"

The boy nodded.

"What made you say he was a man," the chief asked

The boy blushed and looked up at his mother.

"I'm right here, it's alright. You saved everybody's life baby."

With that reassurance, the boy looked back at the fire chief and touched his chest. "Because he didn't have no chee chees."

The fire chief took a moment to process that he meant breasts. "He came to his feet, laughing, looking at the mother, who was also smiling.

"Thank you for letting him talk to me this was a big help. We'll be sending the Red Cross to make sure everyone's taken care of; we just want to make sure everyone is safe." The fire chief turned to the fireman standing in arm's reach. "A man dressed in black, setting off the fire alarms and there's no fire has to have something to do with this whole situation." His colleague nodded in agreement as they both turned to walk towards building three.

The mother picked up her son and hugged him. "You did a good job using your words baby, mama is proud of you. Your daddy's gonna proud of you too when he comes from work."

The boy waved to the fire chief.

The battalion leader tipped his hat and moved towards building three. The fire crew had connected their hose to the water hydrant right in front of the courtyard working until the fire was out. Three hours passed before they were able to get to floors nine and ten that had been blocked off in the third building.

"Chief, you need to get up here," radioed one of the firemen on site on the eighth floor. I think we've uncovered something. Get up here as soon as you can."

CHAPTER 32

Sean still had not revealed his cover as the police were questioning him and every girl that had been brought in from the motel. Sean had heard Sophia yelling from across the parking lot, "All three of them was in on it. Don't let they ass go." As she stepped up into the paddy wagon. "They was helping them take us outta town."

He didn't know where Vik was, and that was not a good thing. His whole goal was to bring Vik down after he rescued Hadassah. He didn't know what happened to the bodies of Auntie Nessa, Tiny and Benny T.

The police chief had called in psychologists and assigned some officers to look up the names of each girl and others to go through missing persons reports.

Sean was sitting in a room alone when his commanding officer walked in. He made sure the door was closed and locked before he began speaking. He smiled "Good work Colton. I'm really glad you found your niece. Dude, I don't know if you really know how huge this is. Some of these girls have been missing for more than five years."

The gentleman walked over to him and fist bumped him.

"So do you know where Batista is?" asked the commander.

Sean was still on the metal bench with his head against the concrete wall. "After I talked to him and had him send the guy driving the other van to pick us up in the park, he didn't contact me again."

"Al is his cousin; he should be able to give you some insight on his whereabouts. He's from Louisiana, that's where we were headed with the girls.

"That might take a while," he snickered "Those girls put a Westside whooping on his ass. He can't talk through that swollen mouth or see out of either of his eyes."

Sean joined in on his laughter. "They were about to attack me too, but my niece convinced them I would help them catch Vik since I was new."

"Smart girl," he replied, "smart girl."

Sean leaned forward, resting his elbows on his knees. "If Batista was going anywhere, he would be the safest with his father down in Metairie."

"This is going to be a long night. Get comfortable. We need to find housing for some of these girls and try to put a trace on Batista. He turned to leave the room, then suddenly faced Sean.

"By the way Colton, your strategy was top-notch. Having your niece tell the waitress to call me and not getting caught with that burner phone was brilliant."

"Truth is, I didn't have her do that. She did it all on her own. In fact, she gave me the thermometer that I stuck in the tire to cause a flat. Her quick thinking slowed us down. I'm so damn proud of her." He softly clapped his hands together.

The Commander's smile never left his face.

"One more thing, I had my clerk bag your weapon and lock it in the safe in my office. Since it was discharged, we'll have to write up a report. I gotcha though."

"Okay cool, I understand. I'm not worried about all of that right now. Can you do me a solid and send in a lawyer to make sure my niece goes home in the next hour?"

"You got it, I'll make a call right now. She'll be ready to go in the next thirty."

"Solid." Sean held up a fist towards the commander and let out a heavy sigh.

"You may as well get ready to choose a desk by the window; you just got a big ass promotion." The smile across his face said it all.

CHAPTER 33

*H*adassah was beyond tired of the questioning. Some of the girls had told the officers she was Vik's main girl, which increased the interrogation time.

"I was snatched up in the park on my eighteenth birthday. I've missed prom and graduation. I've been away from my family for almost three months. How the hell can I be someone's main girl?" she retorted to the female detective sitting across from her at the steel table. She said nothing about Vik's home in suburban Westchester and denied every accusation of her being his main girl. Her uncle taught her the art of not talking too much and therefore she didn't say anything after her last statement.

The tall ebony-skinned woman with a precision cut auburn bob opened the door and walked in without breaking her stride. Her two-piece, fitted black skirt suit and red bottom shoes spoke before she did.

"I'm Jill Nielsen, attorney representing Hadassah Colton. She's done answering questions and unless you're charging her with being a victim of Viktor Batista and his sex-trafficking ring, she needs to be released." She placed her leather briefcase on the table and stood with arms crossed, waiting for the officer to exit the room. The detective closed the file, stood slowly, giving the attorney a once-over eye-roll as she left.

Hadassah breathed a sigh of relief and opened her mouth to ask a question. Jill held up her hand to stop Hadassah with a slight smile. "I was sent by your uncle. We'll talk later after you're released. Sit tight while I get you processed. Your family is outside waiting for you." She picked up the briefcase and left the room. Hadassah lowered her forehead against her arms crossed on the table and held back the welling tears. The thought of seeing her grandmother for the first time stirred her emotions.

Some of the girls began leaving as they were reunited with their families; crying and laughter could be heard throughout the station.

When she laid eyes on her grandmother and her uncle Louis, she let go of everything she had been holding since the day she was taken. Her grandmother shed equal tears of grief and relief. "I'm sorry baby, I'm so sorry we wasn't watching out for you in the park that day."

Hadassah was so overwhelmed with emotion that her uncle picked her up and carried her to their SUV. They had made it home before she was able to speak. Her grandmother had sat in the back seat with Hadassah's head resting on her lap and let her cry, rubbing her back and shoulder. Her uncle, in his wisdom and patience, waited until they were behind closed doors and everyone was seated before he spoke.

"We know all about it was you who gave that message to the lady in the truck stop when you went to get the food. We're so proud of you. Your uncle Derek is going to be fine.

He's not ready to give up his cover yet because those men haven't been found. We just want you to relax and talk whenever you're ready." She hugged her uncle, then Mama Betty.

"Grandma, don't blame yourself. It wasn't your fault; none of this was your fault. Those men had been doing this for years." She gently wiped her grandmother's tears.

"I love you grandma. I was praying the whole time and asking God to help me get out, just like you taught me to and God heard me. I'm just glad to be home." She gave the older woman another hug before laying on the couch and adjusting the pillows under her head.

Her thoughts drifted to Sam. *It was because of her taking her own life, that she and the other girls were saved.*

"If only she could have just held on a little while longer," she whispered.

CHAPTER 34

"Thank you. Thank you all, it was a team effort." Cameras flashed from every side of the room, capturing smiling images of her hero, her uncle Derek; holding his award for bravery and his promotion.

Hadassah beamed, sitting between Mama Betty and Uncle Louis. Several people shook her grandmother's hand or nodded in her direction congratulating her on her heroic son. Hadassah thanked God every day for answering her prayers to be saved from the clutches of Vik's operation.

Not only had Derek Colton rescued his niece and sixteen other kidnapped victims, he had exposed several city and state officials who had been patrons of the Bayou. Derek had been promoted to the Assistant Director of the Sex Trafficking division. With his new authority, he was more determined than ever to bring Viktor Batista to justice.

* * *

"Mr. Colton, the plane is ready and waiting for you and the team at Midway airfield. The pilot is asking what's our arrival time." Derek looked up from his laptop, "Let the team know

we're leaving in thirty minutes. Our scheduled arrival time is ten pm."

He closed the laptop, placing it in a leather crossbody on the edge of his desk. He handed his assistant a sheet of paper as he stood. "Here's our itinerary including the three hotels. Scan it to our contact in Baton Rouge. The plane ride is only two to three hours."

The Louisiana air was humid even for ten o'clock at night. The team stood in a circle waiting for their instructions. "Team one, you're leaving now, team two, thirty minutes behind them and my team, thirty minutes after that." He wiped a sweaty brow.

"Big Vik is heavily connected. We don't want to give any alerts that we're here. We know why we're here and who we're looking for."

He adjusted his bag. "Remember tonight we're moving nice and easy, looking and listening. Our first briefing is 0800 at team three hotel. Enjoy yourselves tonight. Let's move out."

The Colton family was finally settling down after all that had happened. Hadassah being rescued, uncle Derek being promoted and now on a mission in Louisiana to find Vik and extradite him back to Chicago, to face charges.

With a 4.7 GPA, Hadassah received her high school diploma without having to complete any further coursework. She spent most of her days reading and staying in the house close to her grandmother and uncle.

"Baby," Mama Betty said to Hadassah after she could no longer ignore her fear of going outside. "I know you really didn't like that therapist too much, but you have to start talking to someone. You haven't gone past that front porch for two months now." She sat next to her on the sofa.

"I know grandma. I'm just not ready. I know you've been watching me and worried about me. But when I'm ready to go out, I'll let you know." She touched her grandmother's hand. "How's your blood pressure today?"

"You know Shuga. Whatever that potion is you keep making me is doing wonders. The doctor said my pressure hasn't been this under control in years." Hadassah smiled.

"Good to hear, now that we've changed your diet and have you on a mostly plant regiment. You're gonna keep getting better and better."

Mama Betty moved to the edge of the sofa, waved a pointed finger in the air. "As a matter of fact. Since ya' Auntie Ruthie been eating those meal preps you make for her and been drinking them juices, you make in the blender, her diabetes been under control too." A grin spread across Hadassah's face.

Her grandmother was now standing. "Baby, I think you're on to something here. Have you thought about starting a lil' small business? I mean, it seems like you have everything you need in that book you use." Mama Betty had one hand on her hip and the other on the fireplace mantle.

Hadassah sat back and crossed her legs with a chuckle.

"A business, grandma? What kind of business? I'm just using the recipes in the book I kept from Auntie Nessa." As the words left her mouth, the memories of being in the Bayou started flooding back. Her eyes teared up as she stared blankly out of the window.

Mama Betty noticed her sudden sadness and sat close to her, wrapping her arm around her shoulder for a hug.

"I didn't mean to trigger you." She pulled her arm down and cupped Hadassah's hand in hers. "I've just been thinking about all the ways you've been teaching everybody in the family how to eat, and about oils and how to take better care of themselves. Everybody's doing good. Look at the weight them twins done lost. We almost can't call them Weeble and Wobble no more." They both let out hearty laughs.

Mama Betty playfully tapped her granddaughter's knee as she stood.

"Let me just say this and I want you to listen with your heart, not with your mind. It was a terrible thing that happened to you. But you know what, my Hadassah, you are the daughter I never had, and the Lord knew I was gonna be sick the rest of my life if we hadn't found you. And I want you to remember one thing. You made it to the other side; you came back to us. Three of the girls you told me about didn't."

A tear quickly ran down Hadassah's cheek; she didn't bother to chase it.

"Everything that happened to me when I was still down south picking cotton, I used it to help me find my way when I came north." She leaned against the fireplace and lightly tapped her fingertips together. "I used it all, the good, the bad and everything in the middle. It all helped me make it through and survive until I met your grandfather." She was now facing the fireplace and traced a finger across the face of her deceased husband.

"Remember what your uncle said. Tell the story, don't let it tell you. Let's talk some more tonight. You okay with that?" She had now turned back to Hadassah, her eyes glossy.

Hadassah nodded with a big smile. "You know what grandma, you're right. I don't mind talking about it tonight. I sure would like to hear how you used your experiences to move on."

Her grandmother suddenly bent over laughing, with her hands resting on her knees.

"I hope you're ready, cause some of it gon' shock you about Mama Betty." She was still laughing when Hadassah stood to hug her.

"I think I'll be ready."

"Well okay then, let's gon' 'head and get these greens picked."

After all the food was prepped and simmering in the oven and on top of the stove, Hadassah went to her room. Taking Auntie Nessa's recipe book and her notebook from her drawer she propped herself up against her headboard with her knees up, placing the book on her thighs so it faced her. Auntie Nessa's last words, took their place in the forefront of her mind "Make sure everybody goes free." In that moment, she realized she had not *freed* herself. She thought of her grandmother's words and made a note to look up how to start an LLC.

She was no longer a prisoner in the Bayou, yet she was still holding *herself* hostage. Hadassah wondered what the other girls had been doing since they were all set free and allowed her mind to open to the things her grandmother said. The realization was right before her, it was going to take her putting in some internal work and facing up to her fear of thinking about the past. She had to made the decision to no longer live as a victim.

"But how can I use the things that happened to me in the Bayou to improve my life?" She was speaking out loud. Her head rested against the headboard; with closed eyes, she traced her fingers across the cover of the book and up and down the spine. She heard Auntie Nessa's voice clear as day, as if she was speaking to her from the pages.

"You've already started, Dark and Lovely, just keep going."

She opened the book to Sam's note. No one had seen her grab it in Vik's office when the commotion started.

She said in a whisper, picturing Sam's pretty face.

"Yes, my sister. Today, I too, am free."

REDEMPTION

The sound blasted into Ava's ears and sent the first-floor emergency room into total chaos.

Why is everyone screaming and running in slow motion?

She slowly turned in a circle, watching as nurses, doctors, and patients took cover under countertops, and others took cover behind desks, chairs, and gurneys.

Why are the police pointing their guns at me?

Ava's mind became clouded with visuals of every crime television show she could recall. Ones where innocent people paid the price for overzealous officers wielding guns with bullets that didn't have a direct target's name on them.

Why aren't they trying to find the shooter?

She tried to process everything.

Her mind and body were rolling through this scenario as though she'd become part of a black and white movie reel, frame by frame.

Why does my left hand feel so heavy?

Ava glanced down and the silver glint of the gun in her blood-stained hand twinkled as though signaling the only answer that mattered. She released her finger from the trigger. The gun took an eternity to travel from her hand to the bright white tiles.

The moment the metal clattered on the floor, the world became normal once again.

Ava could now hear everything clearly. Screams trailing into sobs. The woman barking orders through the overhead speaker.

Understanding was still a little slow in coming as an officer roughly grabbed her arms from both sides. In a simultaneous, quick motion, both male and female officers, each kicked one of her shins, pulling both feet from under her. She went down, her right cheek striking the cold floor. Pain shot up her head, and she saw stars, and not the kind that signaled a romantic night.

The burly male officer on her right jammed one of his knees into her back, while the female officer pulled her wrists together. The cold metal clicked into place and soon the tightness that bound them caused Ava to stiffen with fear.

What the hell just happened?

Ava cried, realizing that trying to explain to the police and triage clerk about the horrible experience that had transpired a few hours ago had fallen on deaf ears. Through uncontrollable sobs, the words came in a stilted fashion, recounting the details of what happened in that basement. Only three souls were there. Two of those were now damaged—body, mind, and soul. One she hoped was having a conversation with their maker.

Now she was on the floor, screaming with pain that kept shooting from her jaw to her brain. The portly officer's knee was digging into her side, all while cold metal restraints circled her wrists, tightening as she tried to break free.

"You're hurting me, get off me," Ava pleaded with the officer who held her down. Her rib cage bore the brunt of his weight, and his left hand pressed hard against her right shoulder as though she was still a threat somehow.

"Stop resisting," he commanded in the familiar words that proceeded the deaths of several innocent people. "You have the right to remain silent. Anything you say—"

"Get off me," she screamed. "What are you talking about? You're hurting me! I haven't done anything."

Tears blinded Ava because of the intense pain. She turned her head towards the officer, taking in deep breaths after he finally complied, only then was she able to relax her handcuffed wrists against her buttocks. She scanned the expectant faces of the patients and hospital staff looking back to her with wide-eyed curiosity. She searched for someone to help her, anyone who could explain why she had suddenly become the criminal instead of the man who had tried to do despicable things and believe he would get away with doing so.

She caught sight of a large pool of blood surrounding a man who was stretched out on the floor as if he was taking a nap in the middle of the frantic movements of those around them. Two emergency room attendants inched forward, then lifted him onto a gurney, trying to navigate the area without tracking the red sticky substance any further. A blonde nurse climbed on top of the body and pressed her stacked hands into the unmoving patient's chest in quick up and down motions. Another nurse moved a silver pole with a clear liquid IV attached. She managed to stick a needle in his arm, her steps perfectly timed to keep moving right alongside the medical transport.

The head of the person on the gurney was turned in such a way that Ava couldn't see his face.

Ava closed her eyes against the salty, heavy tears that poured down unchecked because the handcuffs didn't give her the opportunity to wipe them away. The nurse shouted commands to the patient who was covered in so much blood there couldn't be any left in his body.

"Come on, stay with me," the nurse pleaded. "Can you hear me? Can you hear me? Come on people, speed it up. We've got to get this man to surgery STAT, we're losing him."

"Let's go, get up."

An officer on each side of Ava, pulled her up through the openings of her arms. She winced at the tightness of the handcuffs as their "assistance" was less than gentle.

"You have the right to remain silent," one officer declared, pushing Ava down the long hallway, speaking the terms that were familiar and ending with, "Do you understand these rights as they have been read to you?"

Everyone in the emergency room stared and pointed at Ava, those waiting to be seen and those who had seen too much. She shook her head, still trying to process what happened. Basement. Pain. Hospital. More Pain. Laughter. Rage.

"Do you understand?" the male officer repeated.

"Understand what?" Ava snapped. "Why am I handcuffed? What are you doing? I came because those bastards were getting ready to rape us." Then another thought swept through her mind.

Oh my God, where's Terri?

She scanned the area, which was now bustling with activity once again, in search of her friend.

The male officer jerked her arm again, harder this time. "I said, do you understand what I just said to you? Do you understand?"

Tears gave way to panic, with thoughts that she would feel this way for a long time.

"Miss, calm down," the female officer suggested above a whisper. "Just let my partner know you understand your rights."

The softness in the woman's voice created a small source of

comfort. Ava angled her head, glaring at the female officer directly in the face "What's happening? What did I do? Where's Terri?"

The male officer nodded to his partner. They made Ava, who somehow became a perp, walk toward the sliding glass doors that lead to freedom for some, but was the beginning of hell for her.

A few steps in, Ava took in the large pool of blood on the floor, then flickered a gaze to the female officer. "Whose blood is that?" Ava inquired, panic lacing her voice. "Is it Terri's?"

"No, it's Alvin Murray's," snapped the male officer as he guided her forward. He leaned in close to her ear with a harsh whisper, "You might know him as Monty. Now keep moving, we need to get to the station." His voice raised two octaves louder.

Ava shook her head, her feet felt as though one hundred pounds had been added to them.

"No, No, No, this can't be right."

She quickly replayed the scene in her mind. The loud boom, then everyone ducking and taking cover. She blinked a couple of times, lowered her gaze, and the rest of the story unraveled with each step.

Penny's invitation. The party. The basement. His attempt to rape them. The blood. The pain. The handcuffs.

My God, what have I done? And where the hell did I get a gun?

Chapter 2

"Penwood, you have a visitor. Let's go." said the stocky guard standing at the cell door with keys jingling on his hip.

Ava stiffened at the sound of her name. She was well aware that Ms. Dot was about to lay down every card in her hand to win the game. Two-hand solitaire was one of the many past times they had in their cells in the afternoons before dinner. Ms. Dot had a particular way of holding her mouth when she believed she had the upper hand and was about to smack down for a victory.

"I do?" Ava questioned the hefty guard, glancing up from a milk crate perched near the metal bunkbed. "I wonder who's here to see me."

Ava looked over to Ms. Dot as she stood and used a foot to move the crate closer to the wall. "My mama just came two weeks ago."

This must be urgent as visitors normally came in the morning.

"Girl, fix ya hair," Ms. Dot cautioned, giving her a toothy grin while stacking the cards into a pile. "Put some grease on your mouth. It might be a sexy man."

"Ms. Dot, you're funny," Ava said with a chuckle, then gave it a little thought. "But I will put a little shine on my lips. I don't know about that sexy man part, though."

Ava snatched a small container from under her bunk, dipped her middle finger in for a dime-sized portion. She rubbed the remaining gloss in her palms, then used it to smooth her dark, unruly hair. "Whoever it is, I don't want to be looking too rough. Might scare them off."

Ms. Dot gave a hearty laugh as Ava stepped to the bars and waited for the guard to turn the key.

The underlying stench of musk and bleach faded the second she stepped into the visiting room. A new scent wafted her way. Strong, but not too heavy. Manly, and not overpowering. Expensive for sure, and certainly nothing like the cheap Brut and Old Spice the guards wore in Dwight. Her gaze locked on perfection. Dark brown suit, broad shoulders and even with his pants almost covering the shoes, she could spot that spit-shine a mile off. He towered more than six feet, and commanded attention even before he parted those luscious lips to say a word.

Good Lord, who is this man right here?

Ava didn't say a word. Instead, she waited for him to look up from the document he was reviewing. With her right hand down to her side, her index finger slid up and down her thumb starting at her fingernail to just behind the knuckle. A nervous habit she still hadn't managed to break. Maybe Ms. Dot wasn't the only one who gave herself away with certain movements.

When he finally turned and locked gazes with her, Ava's breathing hitched. That deep, rich complexion covered a handsome face that was regal, smooth, and polished. He extended a hand with a braided gold band on his middle finger; she took note of the ring not being on his marriage finger. *As if walking down the aisle is anywhere in my future.*

His stealth presence alone was an outward sign that he had his life together. Ava's had fallen apart that one fateful night in Monty's basement. Every day she imagined if her choices had gone a different way —she refused the invitation, went to college, and right now she's an architect.

She accepted his hand as he said, "Hello, Ms. Penwood. My name is Khalil Benson. I'm here from the Innocence HUB in Chicago."

Ava heard only half of what he said and none of what it meant as she stared into his eyes, mesmerized by the smoothness of such a deep voice, and the intensity of his gaze. His strong, but gentle grip sent shivers through her body. *It might be a sexy man.* It looked like Ms. Dot knew something Ava didn't.

"Ms. Penwood?" Khalil repeated.

Ava blinked, breaking her gaze, finally releasing his hand. "I'm sorry, hello."

"Let's have a seat." He extended an arm to the steel bench as he waited for her to comply.

Ava eased onto the cold, hard seat as she admired the taste and fit of his garment. Pale yellow shirt, brown tie, red and beige houndstooth pattern.

"As I said, Ms. Penwood, I—"

"Ava," she asserted. "You can call me Ava."

"Alright, Ms. Ava," he shot back, smiling in a way that showed that he still wanted to keep a professional distance.

She smiled back and inhaled, realizing that this exchange was already the highlight of her day. Most days were filled with arguments, fights, making the best of the chow hall food, and long stretches of empty time.

"I'm here from the Innocence HUB." Khalil extracted a folder from a thin leather briefcase and placed it on the steel table. "We've recently received some information that sheds a different light on your case."

Ava placed both elbows on the table, bracing herself against the smidgen of hope those words and his presence pressed on her heart.

"What do you mean, a different light?" Ava inquired. "What kind of information?"

"I'm going to cut right to the chase because we don't have much time." Khalil flipped open the folder and extended a page her way. "It looks like Cook County Hospital may have been responsible for Alvin Murray's death. Meaning, he may have died from the hospital's negligence, and not the gunshot wound as they said when you were convicted."

In two blinks, her eyes went from being misted to salty, blinding tears. She wiped them away with the sleeve of the orange, cotton Department of Corrections shirt.

"So, what you're saying is my gunshot really didn't kill him?" Ava asked, her voice trembled as she fought to keep her emotions in check.

"That's what it looks like," he replied, flashing a smile. Ava could swear she heard a little song behind that one action. "We have some leg work to do, but the main piece of information is in our possession. In my remaining time here, I need you to tell me exactly what happened that night in the emergency room that led up to the shooting."

Ava inhaled, trying to process that first bit of information.

I didn't kill that man. All these years, she had been wracked with guilt. He may have deserved a bullet for what he'd done to her, but killing him was never her intent. Whether it was her plan or God's to send Monty to an early grave, Ava spent the last three years paying that hefty price.

"We have the transcripts of the case," Khalil said, placing a hand over hers. " I know it may be hard, but I really need you to take some deep breaths, close your eyes, and go back to that night in the hospital."

His instructions were slow and precise as he retrieved a yellow legal pad from the briefcase and a silver pen from inside that fashionable suit jacket.

"Why do you want me to close my eyes? "Ava asked.

Khalil shifted his gaze from the tablet to Ava. "The eyes are the organ that our bodies trust the most. So, even with them closed, they tell the body the most truth and that's what I need here. All of the truth, every single detail that you can recall, Ms. Ava."

Hearing Khalil call her Ms. Ava, made her smile again. She felt like he respected her the way she did Ms. Dot. To her, the title denoted how much she cared for the older woman and now Khalil esteemed her in that fashion.

Ava took a deep breath, inhaling the intoxicating scent of his cologne, once again giving her permission to close her eyes and relax her shoulders.

"Are you as comfortable as you can be right now?"

Ava enjoyed the resonance of his voice. Such a distraction. The same voice which had delivered the best news she'd had in a long while.

"Yes, I'm okay."

"Alright. You and Terri Brewer arrived at the hospital, and …"

She winced at the mention of Terri's name. A tear escaped, streaming down her cheek and a few others followed. When his hand covered hers, she exhaled, trying to center herself.

Many things happened while being in the belly of the Dwight penitentiary beast, and she had formed a mental shield to insulate herself. Now, he wanted her to let down those walls and relive the most horrific night of her life. She would have to if he was saying that freedom was on the other side.

"Keep breathing," Khalil commanded, almost whispering. "Continue taking those deep breaths. I'll be right here when you open your eyes."

She allowed herself to relax with the sound of his voice.

"Now, tell me what happened."

OTHER WORKS BY BRIDGETT MCGILL:

Redemption: Book 1 in the Sins of the Windy City Series
How Does Your Garden Grow? Cultivating a Life of Abundance.

How Does Your Garden Grow? Cultivating a Life of Abundance.

The Interactive Journal.

Birthing Purpose: 21 - Day Devotional Journal

The Oil: 21 - Day Devotional Journal

Emerging Queens: Self-Care Journal for Girls

www.ingramcontent.com/pod-product-compliance
Lightning Source LLC
Chambersburg PA
CBHW021716190726
48289CB00008B/2551